'A thoroughly satisfying and enjoyable read.'
JANE AUSTEN'S REGENCY WORLD MAGAZINE

'Julia Golding has a true sense of history, an ability
to lift characters off the pages and to develop a plot
so intriguing that I can't put the book down!'
MY SHELVES ARE FULL BLOG

'A highly enjoyable story with an excellent plot,
a wonderful cast of well-described characters,
plenty of action, a good dose of mystery, and
some satisfying twists.'
ANNE ROGERS, FICTION FILES FOR TOGETHER MAGAZINE

'Cleverly plotted and full of intrigue and suspense.
A real page-turner.'
GET KIDS INTO BOOKS BLOG

JANE AUSTEN INVESTIGATES

The Burglar's Ball

Julia Golding

LION FICTION

Published by
Lion Hudson Limited
Prama House, 267 Banbury Road,
Summertown, Oxford OX2 7HT, England
www.lionhudson.com
ISBN 978 1 78264 345 6
e-ISBN 978 1 78264 346 3

First edition 2021

A catalogue record for this book is available from the British Library

Printed and bound in the UK, June 2021, LH26

Editor's Note

Notebooks containing details of Jane Austen's first investigations were recently found hidden in a trunk stored in the attics of Jane's family home. There are signs that Jane expected her papers to be discovered, for they begin with a warning from young Jane herself.

Warning

Any resemblance to persons living or dead in these case notes is entirely intentional. Names of people and places have been changed to protect the wicked – but you know who you are!

J.A.

Chapter 1

1789

No one who had ever seen Jane Austen in her infancy would suppose her to be born to solve crimes. From her early love of sugar plums, and cleverness in hiding her expeditions into the pantry, her mother declared her far more likely to commit them. However, as Jane would counter, there was no better person to identify the culprit than the thief turned thief-catcher.

Jane was only just settling in to summer at Steventon Rectory after her adventure at Southmoor Abbey. A few weeks had passed, the long hot days were here, and Jane looked forward to a daily routine of avoiding chores, playing cricket with her father's pupils, and finding secret places to read in the shade undisturbed. However, her plans were to receive a rude shock. Little did the postboy know what trouble he was bringing or he might've posted the letter in a bush to save her.

Stolen sugar plum in a dish on the grass, Jane was lying on

the lawn between the long sheets pegged to the washing line, keeping out of the busy gaze of her mother. Mama always had something improving for her daughter to do, be it to carry a basket of garden produce to a neighbour, help make jam, or fold the linen. Not that Jane minded making jam – it was just that books were so much more exciting! She couldn't abandon her heroine now, not when the bandits were about to descend upon her carriage! With a flick of her hand, she waved a wasp away from her pilfered treat and turned the page of the equally delicious novel she was reading. Wonderful: the hero was riding to the rescue! This was heaven.

Abruptly, Cassandra dashed the linen to one side and snatched the book from Jane's fingers, closing the pages on the dark-eyed hero in the midst of his rescue speech.

"Cassandra!" protested Jane.

"Jane! There you are! You'll never guess what's happened!" Her older sister was breathless with excitement. Cassandra was the beauty in the family; her tawny hair fell in glossy ringlets without application of the curling iron, and her fine eyes were much praised in the neighbourhood. Her conquests of smart "beaux" (her term for eligible young men) were bound to be legion in a year or two – or so Jane teased her. As for Jane herself, she often felt like a poor imitation of Cassandra, a second-hand copy, as she had a reddish tinge to her light brown hair, a flushed face, and she'd grown like a beanpole to unfashionable heights, quite towering over the other thirteen-year-olds in the district, both girls *and* boys. If she didn't love her sister so much, it would really have been very vexing to always be Miss Jane, sister of the handsome Miss Austen.

"If I cannot guess, then I will not try," said Jane, biting the sugar plum in half and offering the rest to her sister. She resigned herself to returning to the novel when Cassandra had delivered her news. It was hopeless to try before that.

"Oh, I can't eat plums, not when there's such news to enjoy!" Cassandra thrust a letter in Jane's face. "Read!"

Jane plucked the paper from her fingers and spread it out. The writing was familiar: it belonged to Madame La Tournelle, headmistress of the Reading Abbey Girls' School, where both she and Cassandra had boarded for a while. The script was as showy and loopy as the writer.

> Dear Miss Austen,
> Already three years have passed since I had the pleasure of entertaining you as a pupil in my little school for young ladies. How I have longed to see your sweetly smiling face! I was saddened that you had to leave us so quickly.

"She makes it sound like this was a choice, when it was *she* who turned us out because Father could no longer pay the fees," said Jane.

"Hush! Read on!" urged Cassandra.

> I am holding an end-of-term party to celebrate our modest little establishment. There will be dancing, of course, and I have

the promise of some very good music from professionals. My girls are already going through their drills daily with the dancing master in preparation so that everything is perfection.

The only thing lacking is your own dear presence. How you would grace our ballroom with your elegance! You were quite my most accomplished dancer and I am assured you have only improved since you resided under my roof. It would bring great joy to my heart if your mother could spare you for a week's holiday to enjoy our end-of-term ball.

Yours affectionately,

Madame La Tournelle

"That's odd," said Jane. "Why write to you now?"

"Because she thinks I will be an ornament in the ballroom!" said Cassandra, doubtless swept away by the image of herself dancing a quadrille to general applause.

Jane knew that this invitation to Cassandra was everything she hoped for. There was precious little dancing to be had at a country rectory, unless you were prepared to dance with your brothers or the boy pupils. At sixteen, Cassandra was too old for such company. Jane passed the letter back to her sister.

"You shall go to the ball!" she declared. "And I'll even let you borrow my new bonnet for the journey. But I'll miss you."

"No, no, you goose!" exclaimed Cassandra, pulling Jane up from the ground. "I couldn't possibly go alone."

Jane nodded. "Oh yes, you very possibly could, because I don't want to go."

"Don't want to go! Think of the dresses, the music, the dancing!"

Towed back to the house, Jane stumbled after Cassandra. "Very well. I've thought of them. You go. I'll stay."

"But I want you to be there," Cassandra pleaded.

"Madame La Tournelle didn't invite *me*."

"That was merely an oversight."

"Oh no, it wasn't. Don't you remember how she always disliked me?" Jane said.

"It'll be fun!"

"I doubt that most sincerely."

By now they had reached Mrs Austen, who was bottling raspberries in the kitchen, hands stained murderous red.

"Mama! May Jane and I go to Madame La Tournelle's ball?" Cassandra asked, not letting Jane get a word in edgeways. "It will only cost the fare as she has invited us to be her guests."

Jane marvelled at her sister's bending of the truth. She thought she could rely, though, on her mother's desire to see that no hint of scandal touched the Austen name. Sending two girls off to Reading, a place full of unknown dangers to inexperienced young ladies, was surely beyond the pale?

"Of course you must go," said Mama matter-of-factly. "Indeed, that is most convenient because your cousins are coming to stay and I have need of your room."

"But Mama, aren't you the least bit worried we'll lose our coach tickets, muddy our hems, or get carriage sick?" asked Jane plaintively. These reasons had all been used by her mother to deny her other pleasures in the past.

"No longer. You showed yourself quite capable of travelling home from Southmoor Abbey on your own, Jane. I have no qualms about sending you to Reading with your sister."

Her father came into the kitchen, a book of Latin grammar tucked under his arms. His pupils spilled out on the lawn and turned cartwheels, the energy pent up in the schoolroom struggling through Pliny now released.

Cassandra knew Jane was brewing revolution against Mama's edict so moved quickly.

"Papa, you won't mind us going to a summer ball at our old school, will you?" asked Cassandra, winding her arm in her father's.

The Reverend Austen looked perplexed. "What? Both of my girls off to temptations of town? I can understand how that might entice you, Cassandra, but that doesn't sound like something Jane would seek."

Thank you, Father, thought Jane.

Mother put a cup and saucer in his hand. "Oh, Mr Austen, you must know that if Cassandra was going to have her head cut off, then Jane would demand hers to be cut off too! Besides, I need them both to be gone so I can give their room to dear Mrs Hancock and Eliza."

"But Papa –!" began Jane, just as Cassandra stuffed the rest of the plum in Jane's mouth in a sneak attack. Her words were lost trying to hide from her mother what she was chewing.

"Very well. They may go." Mr Austen stirred a lump of sugar into his cup of tea. "I'll be in my study."

Jane watched her last hope to be spared the humiliation of a school dance disappear behind a closed door.

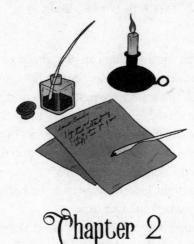

Chapter 2

"I cannot believe you brought that dog with you," sighed Cassandra as Grandison leaped down from the stagecoach.

Jane grinned as her faithful hound loped over to make friends with a sheepdog outside the coaching inn. Grandison was a friendly soul, a disposition reflected in his black-spotted white coat with one patch over his eye. When he sat on his haunches, tongue lolling, it was hard to imagine him anything but happy.

"As you insisted on bringing me on this jaunt, I insisted on bringing him," said Jane, thinking her argument absolutely fair. "At least I'll have someone rational to talk to."

"Oh come on, Jane, cheer up! It won't be that bad," said Cassandra as Jane dragged her feet on the approach to the Abbey School. Behind her, a barrow boy towed their trunk, red-faced with the exertion on this hot summer's day. Cassandra had packed three quarters of it with all her gowns; Jane had managed to squeeze in a measly two – her everyday and her finest for the ball. At the rear came Grandison, too distracted by the exciting new smells to make steady progress forward.

Reading clattered around them in the shape of noisy carters and carriage drivers, street-sellers and schoolboys, horsemen and housewives. The walls were pasted with posters advertising everything from infallible tooth powders to promised rewards for the return of stolen goods. From the looks of it, there was a clever thief at large, as a number of watches and rings had gone missing from supposedly locked rooms.

Interesting, thought Jane, vowing to come back and read the posters properly when she had time.

Cassandra, Jane, boy, and dog processed along the Forbury, the street leading to the school gatehouse. An area of open ground lay opposite the gatehouse, remains of what had once been common grazing land and was now used as a park by the locals. A few magnificent trees had survived even though they were in the middle of town, including a superb oak that reminded Jane of the one that stood in the churchyard in Steventon. The oak was little changed from when they were here three years ago. But then, Jane mused, three years to an oak was nothing in the story of its many rings. The oak was probably here as a sapling when the old abbey was founded. Maybe a monk had planted the acorn?

"Almost there," said Cassandra encouragingly.

"It will be torture," predicted Jane, hopping over a pile of horse manure. "You know, Mama and Papa should have given me your name. I always tell you the future and you never believe me. I'm doomed – like the ancient Cassandra of Troy."

"Fuss-pot!" Cassandra tossed this over her shoulder.

They passed under the archway, the most complete part left of the old abbey ravaged by that cruel and criminal King Henry VIII.

"Greek slavedriver!" retorted Jane.

Cassandra bounded up the steps to the front door of the school. "Crosspatch!"

Jane opened her mouth to come up with a suitable Trojan insult when the door opened and Madame La Tournelle herself hopped out to greet them, a vision of white muslin ruffs and bows, like a puffy cloud fallen to the ground. Memories rushed back to Jane. Madame had never been a friend to her.

"My dear Miss Austen, charmed, delighted to see you again!" she gushed, ribbons on her cap fluttering.

Jane had used the word "hop" advisedly, for stout little Madame La Tournelle had had the misfortune of mislaying a leg at an earlier stage in her career and used a cork one in its place. This gave her a unique rolling gait. The girls had long speculated as to what had led to this unusual state of affairs. Theories ranged from a youthful Miss La Tournelle running away to war dressed as a soldier in pursuit of a beau, thus losing her leg in combat, to her turning pirate like Anne Bonny and sacrificing it in a gun battle at sea. Jane favoured the second explanation, as Madame also had a fondness for her parrot, Don Pedro de Mendez, who was normally to be found fluttering around the gatehouse, screeching challenges as he went on the scavenge for nuts, buttons, or treats left unguarded by foolish schoolgirls. It paid to be tidy at Madame La Tournelle's school and make sure your buttons were sewn on securely.

"Madame La Tournelle." Cassandra dipped a most extravagant curtsey as if she was auditioning to be a lady-in-waiting to the queen.

"Oh, and Miss Jane." Madame La Tournelle's expression became as cold and unyielding as a fire poker. "I had not expected…"

"But I could not travel alone," said Cassandra quickly, "and Jane is my constant companion."

"As Grandison is mine," finished Jane, patting her dog on the head.

"Of course." The headmistress pursed her lips. "I should have anticipated just such a thing. I'm sure we'll find room… somewhere… for her. The dog will have to stay downstairs."

Jane dipped a curtsey of her own, just enough so as not to be insulting. Grandison was unlikely to obey orders, but that was a battle for another day.

"You always said she was the cleverest girl ever to attend your school," said Cassandra.

"Yes, I did, didn't I?" intoned Madame, not sounding at all complimentary.

At this awkward moment, the barrow boy cleared his throat. "Will that be all, Miss?"

Cassandra reached into her purse for his pay, drawing on the coins their father had given them for their expenses. "Please leave the trunk in the hall. The servants will carry it up from there." Jane thought her sister sounded so grown-up. She was proud of her.

"Actually," interjected Madame, "if you would take it to the dormitories. Up the staircase there." She pointed to a palatial wooden structure that had once been covered in gilt but had been worn back to the original oak by years of small hands touching it.

"How many flights, Ma'am?" asked the boy, squinting into the gothic gloom above.

"Two."

"That's an extra sixpence," said the lad, holding Cassandra's gaze.

She narrowed her eyes for a second, then folded. "Oh, very well." She paid him the sixpence and he began huffing and bumping his way up the stairs with the trunk.

Where were the servants? wondered Jane. She remembered there had been several men who did the heavy duties at the school. For that matter, why was Madame answering the door herself?

"If you're not too fatigued from your journey, perhaps you would like to see the preparations in the ballroom?" said Madame, addressing her comment and her concern to Cassandra.

"I would like nothing better," said Cassandra.

Jane and Grandison were not consulted.

Madame led them to the ballroom which took up most of the lower floor of the two-storey school building attached to the gatehouse. Grandison's claws clicked on the flagstone passageway. Jane recalled that above were the chambers where the girls lodged; here was where the schoolrooms with their maps, globes, and magic lantern were located, and the ballroom for learning the most important accomplishments of all: flirting and giggling. *Sorry*, Jane corrected herself, that probably should have been dancing and music, not that she'd come home much improved in either. It was very odd how parents chose to send their girls away to scramble themselves into an education. She herself had learned very little during her time at school, except that she much preferred home.

As they entered the cavernous space, brightened by many tall windows, they came upon a group of the older girls engrossed in learning the steps to a promenade dance. They were listening, with only a few giggles, to an elegant young man with floppy dark hair tied back in a pigtail: the dancing master.

His black jacket and breeches were cut to perfection, though they showed some wear at the elbows and knee buckles, suggesting he lived a life of picturesque poverty (or so the girls would imagine). Jane could immediately guess that he was the current object of the schoolgirls' dreams, as he was handsome and knew how to dance: the two essential requirements for any beau when you are sixteen. Cassandra would doubtless join them in falling in love with him at once.

Not Jane. She was much more interested by the flautist who was accompanying the dance. He appeared to be from Africa, which meant he was possibly a freed slave and now musician for the dancing master. Tall like her, he held the flute delicately in long-fingered hands. His hair was close cropped at the sides but was cut to an inch on top so it sat a little like a coronet. What interested her most though was how his eyes were quick and full of humour; he seemed to be looking on the scene of the bumbling girls before him with the same satirical gaze as Jane.

Grandison wandered over to him and nudged him for affection. The boy patted his head. Jane decided he was a good person on that sign alone.

"Brandon, play that strain again," called the dancing master. "Ladies, you lead with the right arm, not the left. Those of you standing in for the gentlemen, you must remember to do this in reverse on the night."

Not a hope, thought Jane, watching the gathering of fifteen- and sixteen-year-olds trip over each other as they tried a complicated figure of eight. She could already feel her feet tangling in sympathy.

"Mr Willoughby, Mr Willoughby!" called Madame La Tournelle.

The dancing master broke away from his pupils, turned, and bowed. "Madame."

"May I introduce to you the young lady I mentioned, Miss Austen? She was a most accomplished dancer in her time in my school, so I am hoping she will help raise the standard achieved by my girls."

Cassandra, until this point unaware of what was expected of her, gave Madame a confused look. "Indeed, I hold out no such hopes for my dancing."

"Come, come, Miss Modesty, no need for that," simpered Madame, tapping Cassandra's arm playfully. "You must allow me to show the girls what accomplishments they will gain while in my care."

Mr Willoughby bowed over Cassandra's hand. "*Mademoiselle, je suis votre serviteur.*"

"Yes, quite," said Madame. "She'll do very well." It was an open secret that Madame did not in fact speak a word of French, which added to the air of mystery about her origins.

Cassandra fluttered a little to receive the soulful look of this dancing maestro, until recalled to her senses by Jane's sharp kick to her shin. "And this, sir, is my sister, Miss Jane Austen. I'm sure you'll find her equally accomplished."

Jane gave the master a toothy grin. He absolutely would not, but she would let experience teach him this. "Mr Willoughby." She bobbed a curtsey.

"Miss Jane. Miss Austen. Will you join us now?" he asked, sweeping an arm to the class.

"They have only arrived these five minutes past. I'm taking them for tea in my parlour," said Madame. "You'll see them tomorrow. Miss Warren, Miss Marianne, and, oh, Miss Palmer too, would you care to join us?"

Three girls detached themselves from the gaggle.

"Yes, Madame, we'd be delighted," said the eldest and finest dressed of the three.

The five girls followed the hopping madame across the dance floor to the headmistress's private parlour, Jane conscious of the envious looks of those left behind. This was not because the headmistress's company was much sought after, Jane knew, but because her table was the only one in the school that ever saw cake. School food was on the whole wretched, and most pocket money was spent on making it bearable by adding items purchased from the bakeries and confectioners of Reading.

"Cake!" she called to Grandison, perhaps giving the wrong impression as to his name. Her dog's head shot up and he scampered over to her side.

As the headmistress ushered them away, Jane heard the dancing master call out again: "Brandon, from the top. Ladies, concentration please!"

Then the door shut.

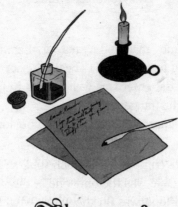

Chapter 3

Jane wondered what to make of the Miss Warrens and Miss Palmer as they sat around the tea table. Why had these three been singled out? Were they parlour boarders? This exalted rank in the school, reserved for the richest girls, spared you the humiliation of taking your meals with the ordinary pupils. Their clothes were certainly fine – sprigged muslin and lots of lace, both of which were expensive items. They also carried themselves with the sort of confidence that went with knowing you were the wealthiest family in the room.

Jane looked around the wood-panelled parlour that had once been so familiar to her. Little had changed, from the funereal cloth painted with tombs and weeping willows tacked behind Madame on the wall to hide the cracks in the plaster, to the row of miniatures above the high mantelpiece. Whom they featured the lady had never revealed. One had a devilish look with black mustachios and a red coat – he was Jane's favourite, so she was pleased to make his acquaintance again. He had often provided the face for the bandit leader or gypsy king in the gothic novels she read.

While Madame made the tea at her little fireplace, Cassandra took it upon herself to begin the conversation at the table. A rector's daughter was well-trained in the tricky art of conversation with strangers.

"Miss Warren, have you been at the school long?" Cassandra asked.

"We're not pupils," said the young lady, providing no further details. She was of an age with Cassandra and had a wealth of wavy hair, the exact colour of a shiny golden guinea. Her nose was pert and her eyes pale blue. She should have been a beauty, but there was something lacking in her expression for Jane. She appeared too placid and without the energy that was needed to animate her features. Her sister, by contrast – a brown-haired girl with brandy-coloured eyes, freckles, and a rounded figure – seemed the sort who would be a good sport. She fidgeted in her seat and looked around the place like a sparrow on a twig, smiling when her eyes met Jane's.

"Forgive me, I assumed you were pupils," said Cassandra.

"But you are almost right," said Miss Marianne, beaming at the Austen sisters. "Father is thinking of placing us at the school. We've recently returned from India, and he wishes to find us a good home because he has to go back to Calcutta."

"Goodness – India! How exciting!" said Cassandra. "So far away. Our aunt lived there for a time."

"And I have a friend from India," offered Jane.

"Oh yes? Perhaps we'll know her," said Miss Warren, showing a little more interest. "Who are her parents?"

"I doubt very much you will have met. Her father is a cook and bodyguard," explained Jane. The one bright spot in the plan to come to Reading was that her Indian friend was currently in the town too. Jane had met Deepti a few weeks ago during her first investigation at Southmoor Abbey, a big house belonging to a noble family. The landowner, Sir Charles Cromwell, had brought Deepti's father back with him from India. Arjun had originally served as a bodyguard for Sir Charles's prized stallion on the long and dangerous journey, but later, once his guarding duties were over and the horse safe in the stable, he had become cook to Sir Charles, who longed for more exotic food than England offered. Arjun's daughter, Deepti, had come with him, leaving her mother and two little brothers at home in India to follow on later when they were old enough to make the voyage. The separation had lasted much longer than planned, because Sir Charles had then gone back on his promise to reunite the family. Thanks to Jane's successful investigation and the prize money Deepti and Arjun had earned, the rest of the family were finally heading for England on one of the next ships from India and were expected to arrive in a few months. Jane knew Deepti couldn't wait for the reunion. For the moment, Deepti and her father were waiting anxiously, reading the news reports and hoping for fair weather for the journey. But Jane wasn't about to explain all of this to strangers. Instead, she kept to names. "My friend is called Deepti," Jane said.

"Oh." And with that one short exclamation, Jane understood that Miss Warren did not know any real Indians but was referring to her acquaintances among the other British people working for the East India Company.

Cassandra hurried to cover the painful silence that followed. "Miss Palmer, are you also recently returned from India?"

This young lady had the peculiar skill of making herself very unremarkable. Jane had not yet had a good look at her, which was unusual as she usually summed people up within a few seconds of meeting them. She now saw that Miss Palmer was a pretty girl, Cassandra's age or a year or two older. She had dark brown hair, and cornflower-blue eyes that were long-lashed and heavily lidded so that you could not see her expression when she had them lowered.

Hmm, thought Jane. This is a sly one.

"No, indeed, Miss Austen. I am just a cousin of the Miss Warrens," Miss Palmer said in a whisper of a voice. "My uncle very kindly offered to place me at school with them so we could become the best of friends."

"And where are you from?" asked Cassandra.

Miss Palmer dabbed an eye with a lace-edged handkerchief. "A village near Bath. My father was a schoolteacher until he died a year ago."

"I'm sorry," said Jane. She couldn't imagine much worse than losing a father. She repented her uncharitable thoughts about Lucy.

"Mother died when I was a baby. Without the kindness of Uncle Warren, I don't know what I would do."

Marianne reached out and squeezed Lucy's hand. "You're among friends now, Lu. No need to worry any longer."

"Tea!" Madame proclaimed triumphantly, bringing the pot to the table. She poured it from a great height but didn't spill a drop, an accomplishment Jane wished the school would teach, as it was much more impressive than anything else on the curriculum. Madame then produced a plate of biscuits that Grandison watched like a Beefeater guarding the Crown Jewels.

"What breed of dog is he?" asked Marianne, scratching Grandison's neck.

"A kind of beagle," said Jane.

Cassandra snorted. "Crossed with a Dalmatian – a Beaglatian."

"Or a Dagle?" suggested Marianne.

Jane actually quite liked that wordplay. "Grandison is a Dagle. Thank you. It is so important to have the right words for things." She took a biscuit and bit into it. It was stale. What was going on at this school? Madame's teas used to be fine things. She dropped the biscuit by her skirt, knowing Grandison would happily clear it up for her. "Did you enjoy living in India?"

"It was too hot," said the elder Miss Warren. "And dusty."

"It is not hot and dusty in Reading," said Madame quickly.

No, they'd be shivering in their cold dormitories come winter, thought Jane, if Madame secured them as boarders.

"I thought India wonderful," said Marianne, her eyes glowing. "The grandeur of the Ganges, the strange sights to be seen around every corner, the temples, the holy men, the native women in their bright silks and cottons. Oh, and the elephants! I adored the elephants."

Miss Warren wrinkled her nose. "If you think that English roads are bad after the passage of so many horses, I dare you to walk down an Indian one."

"Quite," said Madame. "Not an elephant to be seen in Reading either."

More's the pity, thought Jane.

Grandison got up and went to the door, nose pointing at the handle. Jane knew the sign.

"Excuse me, Madame, is there somewhere I can walk my dog?"

Madame frowned. "I don't want any unpleasantness in the school garden."

"Naturally."

"Take him to the Forbury. It's the little green opposite the gateway."

"Yes, I remember."

"You are not to fraternize with Dr Valpy's boys. They play cricket out there," Madame said in explanation to the Miss Warrens, referring to the brother school to her establishment for girls.

Marianne put down her biscuit and got up. "May I come with you, Miss Jane?"

"I'd welcome the company." Jane found a lead for Grandison just in case he took it into his head to run off.

"And don't, whatever you do, leave the door open!" called Madame. "I don't want Don Pedro to get out."

Marianne followed Jane along the corridor. "Don't mind her. Since we arrived, it's happened a couple of times already. That parrot is an expert at escape."

But Jane took care not to blot her copybook with Madame so early on, ushering Grandison out a side door only after she'd taken a suspicious look into the rafters. The parrot had a habit of hiding in the most fiendish places. All clear. She snapped it shut behind them.

Marianne rubbed her hands together with glee. "Excellent. We – and not the parrot – have flown the cage. Fancy a game of cricket?"

Chapter 4

"Do you like playing cricket?" asked Jane.

"I adore it. Our brother – he's actually our much older half-brother as our father was married before – introduced me to the game when we stayed at his home on return from India. That was the first time we'd met Edward."

"The first time you'd met your own brother?" Jane's own brothers came and went with long absences from home, but she could say she met all of them at least once or twice a year. Apart from George. Nobody mentioned George at home. He was feeble-minded, according to her parents, and lived on a farm where he could help with the animals he loved. Jane wondered why he couldn't do that just as well at Steventon. The adult world could be very confusing.

"Indeed. Edward was sent away to school in England before we were born. But he's quite my most favourite member of the family already – just like me in so many particulars – same tastes, same sense of humour. I hope we do end up going to Madame's school because he lives in Reading. He is living in a house near the centre of town and training as a lawyer with a friend of my father."

Jane understood this to mean that there was not a meeting of minds between the elder and younger Miss Warrens, and Marianne was optimistic her brother might fill the friendship gap. "I've a whole clutch of brothers but I have to say I am closest to Cassandra."

"Does she like cricket?" Marianne asked hopefully.

"Yes, when she forgets about trying to be grown-up."

"I know: older sisters can become very tedious. Elinor has to be persuaded to forget her airs and remember to play these days. She's always so serious."

They reached the little green where indeed there was a game of cricket in progress. A boy with a mop of red hair, lanky like a daddy-long-legs, was running up to bowl to a tubby lad with a scarlet waistcoat.

"How shall we introduce ourselves so we can ask them to let us play?" Marianne wondered aloud. Like Jane, she must've decided playing cricket was not fraternizing. Fraternities were for boys only, so therefore they could not be fraternal even if they wanted.

The English language was very useful sometimes.

The scarlet-fronted boy's bat met the ball with a crack and it sailed toward them. Grandison, taking this as his cue, ripped the lead from Jane's hand and bolted after it, beating the fielders handily. He seized the ball and bounded back to the bowler, dropping it at his feet as he had been trained by the boys at the rectory. The bowler snatched it up and tapped the bails.

"You're run out!" he crowed.

The batsman swung his bat in irritation. "That doesn't count. The dog did it."

"He's on our side," said the bowler.

"Since when?" The batsman shoved him.

The bowler shoved him back. "Since twenty seconds ago."

Jane hurried forward before Grandison caused fisticuffs (it had been known). "I apologize for the interruption to play." She took up the lead again. "Bad dog." Her reprimand was half-hearted and Grandison knew it. He sat down and looked happily at his new friends.

The scarlet-waistcoated boy scowled at him. Grandison whined and nudged the bat with his nose, telling him to get on with the game. The boy shrugged and laughed. "All right, I admit it: that dog is a better outfielder than the rest of your team. What's his name?"

"Grandison," said Jane.

"Like the novel?" The boy wiped his brow with his shirt sleeve.

"Exactly. He is a paragon of dogginess, just as Sir Charles Grandison is a paragon among gentlemen."

"Can we play?" asked Marianne eagerly.

Jane sighed. She had been planning on a slow approach to the request, one that was done with the diplomacy required for a group of schoolboys confronted by schoolgirls. Marianne had more the Grandison approach to life: rush in and assume they are your friends.

"You're a girl. You can't play," said the bowler with predictable scorn.

"I can!" Marianne held out her hand for the ball. "I'll prove it to you."

"But this is a boys-only team event," said the bowler. "You aren't welcome."

"You let the dog play."

"He's a boy too, isn't he?"

Jane had to concede he had a point. "Under what

circumstances would you allow us to play?" she asked.

"When the blue sky turns green," said the bowler, thinking himself very clever.

"It does at night under the Northern Lights," she said quickly. She was not to be defeated by a mere technicality. "Therefore, if it goes green tonight – which it will somewhere in the Arctic Circle – we can play tomorrow?"

"Does it really?" said Waistcoat. "How fascinating. I wonder what causes that?"

Jane did not feel qualified to answer. Her father's library was good, but there were some mysteries even his shelves didn't explain. "That remains to be discovered. But will you let us play?"

Waistcoat exchanged a look with Bowler. "You have to bring your own players, because we're not allowed to have girls on our teams," said Waistcoat. "Dr Valpy's orders."

Jane clapped her hands. "Then it is agreed: we find a team and then we can play." She tugged Grandison away. "And by the way, Grandison is on our team. Find your own fielders."

Marianne hurried after her. "But I wanted to play now!"

"That was never going to happen," said Jane sagely. "If I know one thing, it is how boys think. We had to make terms with them. It's like a political negotiation between the Canadian tribes."

Her new friend shook her head. "Political negotiation?"

"Don't you read the newspapers?"

Marianne gaped. Jane took that to mean the Steventon Rectory was a little unusual in what it thought suitable reading material for a girl.

Jane tried another tack. "How do you get your sister to agree to something?"

"I don't. She just ignores me and Father gives her her way. She's the apple of his eye because she's pretty." Marianne tucked her thumbs into her sash and strode along.

"That's a foolish reason to have a favourite."

"She also sounds like him, agrees with everything he says, and loves the same things he does – things like jewellery, fashion, and gossip."

"That would do it then. She is him in miniature, a female edition."

Marianne laughed. "You are right! I hadn't thought of it like that. It is just as well that most of her wishes are ones I don't mind, like trying this school rather than one in London."

"And maybe you are more like Edward, so you get to be the favourite sister of another family member?"

"Perhaps. I certainly don't want to be like my father, love him though I do." Marianne looked about her. "Where are we going?"

Jane sniffed. It was around here somewhere. "I'm hungry so I'm in search of a bakery."

"We're allowed to do that?"

"I've not been forbidden to do this. After all, I'm not a student any longer."

"And I'm not one yet. Thank goodness: the food at school is terrible." Marianne linked arms with Jane. "Lead on!"

The bakery was on Broad Street, not far from the church of St Mary. It wasn't the closest one to the school, but Jane had a particular reason for seeking it out. It was a brand-new secret revealed only in Deepti's last letter. Tying up Grandison to a post near the door, Jane and Marianne entered the shop, bell tinkling. It smelled wonderful – yeasty, sweet, and spicy.

"I wish I could bottle this smell," sighed Jane.

Marianne dug in her pocket. "I have a shilling. A couple of those iced buns perhaps? Oh wait: what's that on the top of that cake?"

"Cardamon pods," said Jane dreamily, her mouth watering.

"Cardamon in Reading? How wonderful. I'd quite given up hope of seeing any ever again."

When the baker turned to serve them, his face wrinkled into a smile. "Miss Jane, what a pleasant sight. Deepti was hoping you would come today. She has been so excited since she received news that you were coming to Reading." He rang a little bell on the counter.

"How are you finding life as a baker, Mr Arjun?" asked Jane.

"It has only been a week but already I find it much less arduous than being the cook at Southmoor Abbey," Arjun admitted. "I like to be my own master." Deepti and her father had recently left Sir Charles Cromwell's employ. The nobleman had received a serious public disgrace thanks to Jane and her friends, so father and daughter had decided it would be wiser to explore a life elsewhere. Setting up as a baker in the biggest local town, offering more exotic treats than the usual fare, was a bold but hopefully profitable step. There were enough rich men returned from serving in the army in India settling in the area to create a demand for his baking.

"How did you manage to get such a wonderful place?" asked Jane, looking around at the bow window displaying the baker's wares, the shelves of loaves, the glimpse of a baker's ovens out the back, chief source of the most delicious smells.

"Sir Charles gave me the funds to make the move here on the understanding I keep him supplied with his favourite dishes." Sir Charles had a taste for the food of the subcontinent. "Lady

Cromwell seconded the idea as it meant she could employ a cook at home more to her liking."

"I'm pleased it has turned out so well for you."

"The timing was fortunate. The old baker was happy to sell up; he had been trying to retire for a few months, since his health began to fail. And I am lucky not to have to start a business from scratch."

Soft footfalls came on the stairs, joined with a little tinkle of tiny bells. Deepti burst into the bakery. The bells were on the ribbons of her bright blue tunic.

"Jane!" She bowed, hands held to her chest. "How wonderful to see you again!"

Jane bobbed a curtsey. "And you, Deepti."

"How do you like Father's new shop?" Deepti spun in a circle to display it, dark plait flying behind her. "Is it not just the top of the trees?"

Jane laughed at the English phrase delivered with Deepti's musical accent. "I like it very well indeed. May I introduce Miss Marianne Warren? She's just come from India herself and I wouldn't be surprised if you find you have a new customer in her, as she is missing the sights and smells of India."

"Miss Warren." Deepti offered an English curtsey.

"How did you two become friends?" asked Marianne, looking between Jane and Deepti.

"I think it was all thanks to ghost-hunting," said Jane, "mixed with a modicum of horse stealing – but not by us."

"Do not forget the house fire," said Deepti.

"And the steam engine," offered Jane. The two friends shared a smile.

"That sounds intriguing." Marianne sounded wistful. Here was another girl who liked adventures, Jane decided.

"I will tell you the full story later, but perhaps we'd better return to school now before they notice we've been gone so long?"

"How may we serve you, Miss Warren?" asked Arjun, taking the hint that his customers were about to leave.

"Cardamon cake, if you please," said Marianne.

"How many slices?"

"All of it," said Marianne, revealing a well-stocked purse. "I think I am about to be the most popular girl at school!"

(Editor's note: enclosed in a letter sent to Henry Austen, a little smeared with cake crumbs from a midnight feast.)

My dear brother,

I enclose our latest school report for your perusal.

Affectionately, your humblest sister, Jane

The Miss Austens' School Report
By the Unstoppable Madame La Tournelle

Cassandra Austen

Deportment – 10/10 – Miss Austen floats around the Abbey School like a petal borne on a gentle breeze.

––

Accomplishments – 9/10 – She delights us all with her playing on the pianoforte, the harp, and the spoons. Her dancing is fit for the highest circles. Her only flaw is that she insists on involving her sister in all her doings.

––

Punctuality – 5/10 – Sad to admit that this otherwise spotless young lady fails to rouse herself in a good frame of mind each morning but grouches until at least ten o'clock.

––

Piety – 8/10 – She is a modest and religious young lady, only let down by allowing her sister to make her giggle during my lectures.

Jane Austen

Deportment – 2/10 – Carthorses move with a lighter tread than the younger Miss Austen. When she isn't galloping along the corridor with that hell hound of hers, she is turning cartwheels in the garden with the younger girls.

Accomplishments – 3/10 – I allow she is a fluent writer but her spelling is atroshush. I will draw a veil over her failure to master the minuet and her tendency to think her singing better than it is.

Punctuality – 10/10 – Jane is allowed one good quality. She is never late, and indeed often surprises me by arriving before time, hoping to catch me unawares.

Piety – 4/10 – She comes from a rectory? How can this be? She giggles at my pronunciation of names in the Bible and was heard to use a bad word at supper.

(Editor's note: this word was "pigswill" and I was referring to the soup. An impartial judge would take my side.)

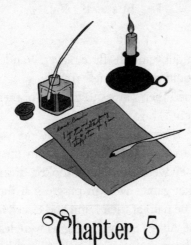

Chapter 5

Over a breakfast of first-rate bread smuggled from Arjun's bakery and greasy school butter, Jane and Marianne had a cricket team meeting. Recruitment for the game was progressing well. In addition to Jane, Marianne, Grandison, and Cassandra, they had also persuaded Deepti, Arjun, and Lucy Palmer to join in. Lucy was always so obliging, said Marianne, and Deepti and her father were intrigued to find out more about this strange English game.

"We really need another four players to be a full cricket eleven," said Jane.

"I'll bring Elinor. She may only look decorative in the outfield, but she'll do it if I tell her she'll be able to examine her prospective partners for the ball among Dr Valpy's boys," said Marianne. "And I'll send for my brother, of course. He can be our chief batsman. All we require now is another two."

Jane considered the people she had met since arriving. They couldn't ask any of the schoolteachers or girls who might report their plans to Madame. Better to seek forgiveness after the event than to break a rule made against it beforehand. "I know: what about Mr Willoughby and his flute player, Brandon? They both look like they could dash off a few runs."

Marianne added their names to the end of their list. "There: that makes eleven."

"We haven't asked them yet. What do you think will persuade them to agree?" Jane got up from the bench in the alcove where they were sitting and looked down on Forbury Green. No cricket games were in progress at the moment, as the boys would be hard at their Latin and Greek in their school next door. In the Abbey School, the girls were learning French – not from Madame fortunately. Their voices chanted away in the room below, reminding Jane that she had let hers lapse. There wasn't much call for French in Steventon.

"I know how to get them to come along." Marianne got out her purse and put it on the table to count out some coins. "I'll engage their services. We'll call it an extra dance lesson."

"Cricket certainly does teach you to be light on your feet." Jane pretended to run backward while positioning to catch a ball that had been hooked into the air.

"And swing your arm elegantly to the right." Marianne mimed using a bat.

"Or overhead." Jane bowled an imaginary ball. "Howzat!"

The girls clasped hands and spun each other in a circle, Grandison barking at their flying petticoat hems.

At four o'clock, the Abbey Miscellany, as Jane had dubbed them, met under the archway. Edward Warren, as Marianne had said, was an older, male version of her, right down to the sprinkle of freckles, brandy-coloured eyes, and enthusiasm. Once introductions were over, he immediately took charge of the motley crew of girls, boys, men, and dog, putting them in their place in the batting order after a brief consultation as to their skills. Edward and Marianne were to open batting, Arjun was to be their fast bowler, Willoughby their wicket keeper. Brandon, who had never played the game, was put near the end of the batting order and told to manage as best he could.

Jane sidled up to him. "Are you happy with that?"

The flautist shrugged, fingers playing a silent, worried strain on his jacket pocket. "I somehow always thought it a good idea to know the rules of a game before you play it."

Jane opened her mouth to explain, realized the task would take a better girl than her, so shook her head. "Trust me, in cricket it is far better to follow orders and muddle through. That's how we learned from our brothers. My name is Jane Austen of Steventon, by the way."

He made her a curt little bow. "Brandon King, late of HMS *Intrepid*."

"That is a sixty-four-gun ship of the line, is it not?" Jane exclaimed. He gave her a surprised look. "I have brothers bound for the navy. We study the lists at home to see where they may end up. Were you a sailor?"

Brandon looked away, over her head, to the cloudless sky. "They would say so. In truth, I was a prisoner."

"I'm sorry to hear it. How did that happen?" Jane had expected him to say he had been a slave, but then again prisoner sounded just as bad.

"I was impressed as an ordinary seaman, but my real duties were to be a musician."

With the permission of the government, the press gang roamed the streets of British ports looking to make up numbers for a crew by forcing men into the navy. Life as a seaman was notoriously dangerous, and sometimes it was very hard to persuade men to sign up with an unpopular or unlucky captain. "I thought only sailors could be recruited that way?"

He laughed grimly. "The press gangs do not care. They heard me play in an inn in Jamaica and decided I would be a useful addition to the crew because their old piper had died of fever while in port. They took me from the street that very night, and I was not allowed to step ashore for six years for fear I would run away."

Jane was shocked, thinking of the little boy hauled off the street by big rough men and thrown on board a ship. It must've been terrifying. "Goodness! You must've been very young?"

"I was about eight. Perhaps it was a better life than the one I would have led in Kingston, but I had no choice either way. I was already a slave. I just switched one master for another."

Jane had heard rumours of the inhuman conditions under which African slaves lived in the Caribbean, but this was her first time meeting someone from there. Until now it had felt a distant wickedness, something about which men in Parliament argued over the rights and wrongs, and not touching Jane's life. It was different to be confronted with a living, breathing person who had experienced the evils of the slave trade. Jane felt very confused and ashamed of her country's part in it.

"But you are free now? You can't be a slave in England, can you?" Jane had always comforted herself with that thought.

Brandon grinned. "I slipped away when we called in at Bristol and earned my bread for a few days playing my flute on street corners. Mr Willoughby found me and took me in as his apprentice. Yes, I am free – for now. There is no slavery allowed on British soil, only in the empire."

Their conversation broke up when Edward Warren gave an

admirable whistle. "Come along, team. I can see Dr Valpy's boys assembling."

Jane and Brandon followed at the end of the line. Cassandra, Jane noticed, was listening very closely to everything Mr Willoughby said about the right and wrong way to catch a cricket ball. Roped into every game since she could walk, Cassandra had years of experience but she hid this in order that, Jane surmised, Mr Willoughby could have the pleasure of teaching her. Mama had always said that it didn't help for a girl to seem too clever (she usually said this with her eyes on Jane).

Waistcoat and Bowler were waiting for them. They now introduced themselves as Tom Thatcher and Michael Redfern, two of the senior pupils at Dr Valpy's.

"We didn't think you'd actually get a team together," said Tom, still wearing his splendid scarlet garment so he looked like the boy version of a robin. "Redfern thought you were joking."

"My sister, sir," said Edward Warren, "never jokes about the things she really cares for."

"And cricket is one of them?" asked Michael. "Capital!"

An older boy from Dr Valpy's offered to umpire, so the team captains faced each other for the coin toss.

"Mr Warren, your call," said the umpire.

"We'll bat first." Edward beckoned his sister forward. "Ready, Marianne?"

The boys sprinkled themselves about the outfield. Seeing that Marianne was to face the first ball, some of them weren't taking it very seriously. They chatted among themselves and one even sat down. Michael tossed the first ball, making it nice and easy for a girl. Marianne swung, connected, and skied it for –

"Six!" shouted Edward. "Oh, well done, sister."

The boys got serious after that and tightened up their attack. No more plucking the grass to make hooting noises on the outfield. Marianne proved she was indeed adept at the game, refusing to fall for the bowler's tricks, keeping up a steady defence of her wicket. She looked set to be there for some time yet.

Having nothing else to do while the first pair were in bat, Jane lay on her back and watched a cloud go by. This was the problem with cricket: there was a lot of sitting around. Normally she'd read but she hadn't brought a book with her on this occasion. Mr Willoughby was entertaining the other girls from the school with his stories, but she didn't feel like listening to his anecdotes about the ballrooms he had known. Deepti was talking to Brandon about sea voyages, but she couldn't catch much of what they were saying. Arjun was also lying down, head resting on Grandison, snoozing after a baker's early start.

Despite her best intentions, Jane couldn't help but hear some of the dancing master's life story he was sharing with his audience, enjoying being the centre of their attention.

"After hearing the great Mr King command the Assembly Rooms in Bath, that was when I knew I had to be a dancing master and perhaps, one day, a Master of Ceremonies like him," said Mr Willoughby to the evident delight of Cassandra, Elinor, and Lucy.

"But of course – you were born for it!" said Cassandra in a rapt tone.

Oh dear, thought Jane. Her sister had succumbed to his spell.

"Though I have no fortune, my natural musicality is wealth enough, or so I reasoned," Mr Willoughby said bravely. "I told my father that I would listen no longer to his demands that I become a man in his image and join the army. So I struck out on my own. I took not a penny from him and have earned my own bread ever since. If killing my fellow man is the price of his approval, then I will continue to decline his overtures of reconciliation."

Jane felt some sympathy for Mr Willoughby. The army life of obeying orders and saluting had little to attract a romantic person. Even life in a military band meant marching to someone else's tune. She did not even want to contemplate what was expected of a soldier on a battlefield in the heat of war. No, if she had been a boy, she would have preferred the adventure of the high seas and exploring the world as two of her brothers had chosen. That was far more fitting to the temperament of an Austen.

Deepti got up to stretch in case she was called in soon to bat.

"What number is Grandison on our batting order?" Brandon asked Jane, nodding to the dog.

"He's our last man," said Jane. "I don't think we've quite worked out how that will go, so I imagine we will declare at that point."

"Declare?"

"Give up the bat to the others."

Brandon followed her example and lay back. "How long do you think the game will last?"

"Oh, cricket can last days."

"Days!"

"Don't worry. We can always pick it up another time if we have to go in for supper," Jane said consolingly.

But another kind of interruption was about to ruin that plan.

Chapter 6

"Don Pedro!" squawked Madame.

Across Jane's field of vision, a red streak passed. She sat up quickly and saw Madame's parrot had made its bid for freedom from the gatehouse as a wagon unloaded. The bird got as far as the oak tree that shaded the cricket pitch. Madame was hot on Don Pedro's trail – and the girls were about to be in big trouble for playing a game against the boys.

"Quick!" said Jane. "Gather round. We're making daisy chains." She grabbed a handful. "Look busy."

"What about Marianne?" asked Elinor, gazing worriedly at her sister exposed in the centre of the field.

"She's with your brother. That should be excuse enough."

Arjun and Deepti, realizing that the cricket team had to blend into the background, walked away to admire the nearest flower bed. Grandison went with them. That left Brandon and Mr Willoughby to sort out.

"You mean you haven't got permission from Madame?" asked Mr Willoughby, aghast that he might lose his best paying customer for daring to join the girls in an unsanctioned game.

"We haven't *not* got permission," said Jane.

Cassandra, used to Jane's ways, swooped in to cover for her. "Mr Willoughby, perhaps you would read to us from an improving work?"

"I haven't got an improving work!" he exclaimed, patting his pockets as if he expected a volume of sermons suddenly to appear.

"You must have something," Jane hissed.

"I have music," said Brandon, passing Mr Willoughby a rolled-up sheet from a flute concerto. Thank goodness someone had some sense.

"That's excellent. You are explaining music to us. Go!" Jane ducked her head and began threading daisies as if her life depended on it.

Mr Willoughby swallowed and began: "Young ladies, music is built on a scale. See here – a scale. And it has notes. See here – lots of notes."

Thank goodness this wasn't a real lecture, thought Jane.

By this time, Madame La Tournelle had reached them.

"Has anyone seen my parrot?" Madame was distraught, not even paying attention to her pupils' activities.

"Oh mercy, don't say Don Pedro has escaped?" exclaimed Cassandra, rather overdoing it in Jane's estimation, as she clasped her hands to her heart in a gesture learned from the family's amateur dramatics.

"I have some nuts, Madame," offered Lucy, holding out a handful of peanuts she'd stashed in her pocket.

"Thank you, Lucy." Madame then realized a good part of her school was sitting on the grass. "Girls! What are you doing here? And Mr Willoughby?"

"We're making daisy chains," said Jane, displaying hers.

"And learning music," said Cassandra with a graceful wave to their lecturer.

Madame frowned. "I suppose that is all very ladylike. But where is your chaperone?"

"My brother is looking after us," said Elinor, proving she wasn't entirely ornamental.

"And where is he?"

"Teaching Marianne how to play cricket." Elinor pointed.

Unfortunately, at that moment, Marianne connected with another short ball and hit it for six.

"Beginner's luck," said Jane, leaping up and applauding. "Oh well done, Marianne!"

Marianne looked over and saw Madame standing among her teammates. She waved the bat jauntily. Edward leaned over and whispered something in her ear, perhaps reminding her that young ladies caught playing cricket should not look so happy about it.

"Do you need help retrieving Don Pedro?" asked Jane, thinking a change of subject imperative. "Perhaps Dr Valpy's boys can assist?"

Following a betraying cackle of joy that came from overhead, Madame hurried off to flutter around the base of the oak tree, as Don Pedro looked down on her with a supercilious beak. Even Lucy's handful of peanuts did not sway him.

"Mr Warren, do you think you can organize a parrot hunt?" Cassandra called.

Edward tapped his forehead in a salute and gathered the bowlers. It was clear the cricket match had to be abandoned because bird stopped play, but happily the boys were game for a new adventure.

Tom and Michael jogged over to the headmistress.

"Madame La Tournelle, shall we climb up?" asked Michael.

Arjun joined them. "I have a scarf you can throw over the escapee." He offered the colourful sash Deepti had been wearing. It glittered with sequins.

"Er, thank you, sir," said Michael. He pretended he hadn't just been introduced to the baker.

Arjun made a stirrup with his hands and boosted Michael into the oak. The parrot fluttered to a higher branch.

"Tricky little blighter, this one," said Michael, pulling himself up another level. "Almost, almost, there!" He threw the scarf over the bird, but Don Pedro launched himself at the same moment and streaked away, scarf fluttering behind him like a phoenix tail.

"After him!" bellowed Madame. The remaining cricketers from Dr Valpy's Eleven ran after Don Pedro, hooting and calling, Madame following as fast as she could manage.

Michael dropped to the ground. "Sorry – I think I lost your scarf."

Deepti shook her head in disbelief.

Arjun stood, hands on hips, looking at the chase in bemusement. "Does this happen often?"

"Don Pedro escape? Oh yes. At least once a week," said Michael with a shrug.

"Do you ever catch him?" asked Jane shrewdly.

"Only the first time. Then he became wise to our strategies. Now, we all have a mighty run around and retire defeated. He flutters home when it gets dark."

Jane wrinkled her brow. "So it is all for nothing?"

"Oh no. It's jolly good fun – and there is always the chance that next time we will catch him."

The last players from the two teams parted for their separate schools, agreeing to resume the game at the first opportunity. The boys were wanting revenge, as Marianne had already scored twenty runs against them, Edward thirteen.

"What now?" asked Mr Willoughby, looking about the gatehouse for sign of another teacher. "It doesn't feel right to depart for home when Madame La Tournelle is absent. I will escort you young ladies inside."

The headmistress returned before he had to make a decision whether or not to leave the school without an adult present to go to his next appointment. Hot and tired, she clomped back inside parrotless.

Cassandra rushed forward with a chair. "There, Madame La Tournelle, you must rest."

Lucy Palmer had dashed to the scullery and returned with a glass of water. "Madame?"

"You are both angels," said Madame. "But what if I never see Don Pedro again?"

Jane suspected the parrot would survive very well indeed so had no fears for the bird's safety.

"He's bound to come back soon," soothed Cassandra.

"He is such a sweet, faithful creature – you must not fear that anything bad will happen to him," added Lucy, "like being run over by a cart or caught by a cat."

This produced more wails from Madame. "Oh, girls! Girls! He is the only thing I brought with me from my life before Reading. I would miss him dreadfully." Madame fanned herself with a be-ringed hand.

A clue to her origins! thought Jane. Maybe she should pay more attention to the bird and find out if it had any words that would betray exactly what Madame had been up to before becoming headmistress?

Elinor now spotted a new delivery in the gatehouse. "Look, Marianne, our trunks have arrived."

"I thought we already had our luggage with us?" asked Marianne.

"I asked Father to send our good clothes and jewels for the ball."

Marianne frowned. "But –"

"I know you are always saying we'll lose them, but they are meant to be worn, not locked away in the family vault." Elinor tapped the lid of a small case sitting on top, made from red Morocco leather with gilt decoration. It looked very expensive to Jane, the kind of casket that jewels and important documents were kept in.

"You had better move those upstairs," advised Jane. "The street door is rarely locked during the day and there's a thief at large in Reading, according to the reward posters."

"I will make sure they are locked in my room. Madame La Tournelle?" said Elinor. "Is there a manservant to help?"

"Oh, what's that, dear?" Madame fluttered her handkerchief in Elinor's direction.

"Our clothes for the ball have arrived. Is there someone who can take the trunk upstairs?"

Madame pulled herself together. "Ah yes. We're a little short-handed at the moment, I'm sorry to say." She cast around for her victim. "You there, boy, will you carry the cases upstairs?" She pointed at Brandon.

"Me?" Brandon looked startled to be singled out.

Mr Willoughby nudged him. "Yes, of course, my servant would be delighted to assist you. Madame, perhaps you would feel more comfortable if I escorted you to your apartment?" He offered the lady his arm and helped her limp to her study.

Elinor, Lucy, and Cassandra followed, all seeming rather too interested in what Mr Willoughby was saying and doing for Jane's liking.

That left Brandon, Jane, and Marianne to consider the heavy trunks.

"Oh, come on then; we'll all help," said Jane, taking a handle of the heaviest.

Marianne picked up the casket. "I cannot believe Elinor asked Father to send these. I wager she's asked for the diamond parure."

Brandon picked up the other end of the trunk. "What is a 'parure'?"

"A matching set – tiara, necklace, earrings, brooch, and bracelet. It was given to our mother by the ruler of Hyderabad in India. It will be far too much for a school ball, where the rest of the girls will be lucky if they are wearing a string of seed pearls. But that's Elinor. Never one to stint on her appearance."

The trunk wasn't as heavy as Jane had feared but she had to pause on the landing.

"I don't even have pearls," she said.

"Don't worry, Miss Jane, I'm sure people will only be looking at the dancing at the ball," said Brandon.

Little did he know women. Balls were an opportunity to price every yard of muslin or silk, every inch of lace and beadwork, and deduce where each person fitted in society. In fact, thought Jane, every lady had a training in being a detective by the very act of noticing these finer details of dress and behaviour.

They reached the top floor. Marianne and Elinor were sharing the best room in the establishment, which had a grand view over the Forbury.

"Oh look! There's Don Pedro, sitting in that tree!" said Jane, standing by the open window. "And that's Deepti's sequinned sash fluttering beneath him."

Brandon and Marianne joined her.

"Should I try to catch him?" asked Brandon, not sounding too keen.

Jane studied the crafty stance of the parrot. He looked primed to fly off as soon as anyone approached. "I think it is best left to the parrot to decide when to return."

"Poor Deepti's sash won't be the same again. We'll have to pay her for it," said Marianne. "I'll send her the money for a replacement."

"Indeed," said Jane with a chuckle. "When she put it on this morning, I imagine she had no idea it would be stolen by a parrot and become its nest by the end of the day."

Chapter 7

A few afternoons later, Jane sat at the edge of the ballroom and wondered how many more excuses she could come up with so as she wouldn't have to dance again. While she was a passable dancer in Steventon among friends and family, thrown into the midst of strangers in Reading any natural ability had flown out of the window. She really did have all the elegance of a carthorse, as Mr Willoughby had been heard to mutter. That insult had not done her already tender confidence any favours, and her insides were squirming with embarrassment. She felt too tall and too awkward. Still, she had to honour the Austen name and pretend that she was not offended. Therefore, she did her best to wear her most impassive expression and ignore the pupils' sniggering and sideways glances when she set foot on the dance floor.

This was not the summer holiday she had imagined – humiliation and public exposure in town, instead of peaceful reading and secret writing in countryside retreats. She vowed one day to get her revenge on the dancing master. She wasn't sure exactly what she would do, but it would probably involve making sure no one by the name of Willoughby was ever looked on favourably again.

Feeling defeated, Jane let her shoulders slump and her back curve in a way her mother would be quick to reprimand. The thought made Jane homesick. Things had to be bad if even her mother's sharp words were something she missed. If her father were here, he would tease her and bumble about the dance floor so that by contrast she felt as nimble as a fairy – that would cheer her up. Her brothers would tell her to buck up and do her best. But Mama, Papa, and her brothers were miles away in their quiet little village; there was no one on hand to help her face the humiliation of failing before all the girls of her own age. If Cassandra weren't clearly enjoying herself so much, Jane would really be on the next coach home. The things she did for her sister!

Grumpily, she rubbed her ankles. Her feet were hurting in her dancing slippers, as the practice had been going on for hours. Looking across to the musicians, she saw that even Brandon looked tired, rubbing his mouth as he was asked to repeat the same refrain over and over. Mr Willoughby was putting them all through their paces, as if their lives depended on their standard of dancing at the ball. The triumphant prodigal, Don Pedro, perched on the rafter and cackled like a maniac, adding to the general air of desperation.

The only two girls not fatigued by the constant repetitions were Elinor and Cassandra. Mr Willoughby was using both as his model pupils, Elinor for her elegant bearing and Cassandra for her nimble steps. Both beauties glowed beneath his praise.

Oh heavens, thought Jane glumly. Cassandra was going to fall in love with him if she hadn't already, as she did any handsome young man. When they finally left Reading (*hooray!*), Cassandra would be saying, "Mr Willoughby this" and "Mr Willoughby that", until Jane would become quite sick of it and for ever she would have only bad associations with an otherwise unremarkable name. She knew that lay in her future as sure as eggs were eggs.

Then Jane noticed Lucy Palmer looking on from the edge of the room. Her rapt expression suggested another girl who was not yet tired of every word that fell from the dancing master's lips.

Marianne slumped next to Jane. "Lawks!"

"I know exactly how you feel." Jane slipped her foot from her shoe and massaged her toes through her cotton stocking. She made her confession. "In case you haven't noticed, I'm not a natural dancer."

"Neither am I." Marianne didn't even pretend to flatter Jane.

"But I am the worst," Jane admitted. "I seem to have lost all ability to count in time to the music."

"It doesn't help that you mouth the numbers the whole time and frown like a gorgon."

Marianne didn't pull her punches, Jane decided. But was her dancing really as bad as that?

"But I can dance at home – really I can."

"Of course you can," said Marianne, not sounding convinced.

Jane did have one solace. "But have you noticed, Marianne: there is one big flaw in this whole undertaking?"

"There is?"

"While we are being drilled like new recruits bound for the front line of battle, do you think anyone is telling Dr Valpy's boys what to do when mustered?"

Marianne giggled. "Oh, that is priceless. I'm going to enjoy this now, us looking relatively proficient while they stumble through the moves. We'll beat them on the dance floor as we did on the cricket field."

"Relatively proficient" was several rungs above where Jane was aspiring; her aim was on "not a complete disgrace". She wondered aloud, "Unless Mr Willoughby is spending his evenings next door showing them what to do?"

Marianne frowned. "I can't imagine those boys agreeing to sacrifice all their spare time, can you?"

"In my humble opinion, it is too late for any of us. The ball is tonight, so if we haven't learned the steps by now, then there is no hope." And certainly no hope for her. A conveniently twisted ankle might be her only escape. Would Cassandra forgive her if she did that?

The practice ended early so the girls had time to have dinner and dress for the evening's entertainment. Unlike other practices, Madame had been noticeably absent from rehearsals today. Intrigued, Jane went exploring and spotted the headmistress engaged in the lowly task of making sandwiches and other nibbles for the cold supper that was to be served. She stood in the kitchen buttering bread while the cook made the school dinner, the two women chatting in broad London accents rather than the refined drawl Madame adopted before her clients. The scarcity of staff for a ball confirmed Jane's deduction that Madame had let go all but the most essential workers. There was still a matron who looked after the girls at night, but no manservants to do the heavier tasks. In the kitchen, as far as Jane could see, Cook was assisted solely by an overworked scullery maid, but that was it – far too few servants to service a whole school. Even her parents in their little rectory had more household staff. Teachers came into Madame's school to give their lessons, but none were employed full-time as they had been in the past. Jane's conclusion? The school was in deep financial trouble. No wonder Madame was so desperate to land the Warrens with their fine clothes, diamond jewellery, and rich father.

As she wandered back toward her room, she came across Brandon feeding peanuts to Don Pedro in the entrance hall. It was rare to see him without the dancing master in attendance.

"Have you been abandoned here by Mr Willoughby?" she asked.

Brandon flashed her one of his quick smiles. "He went for a walk with some young ladies and told me to wait for him. I think he preferred to have their attention for himself."

That confirmed Jane's opinion that the man was essentially a peacock. She sat on the bottom step. "Which young ladies?"

"The elder Miss Warren and her cousin. I think your sister also accompanied them."

Jane nodded. That made sense, though she was a little hurt Cassandra hadn't invited her along. Maybe she had taken Jane's moans about sore feet seriously? Added to that, Jane had not tried to hide her disdain for Mr Willoughby. Her presence would have dampened the self-congratulatory mood of the walking party. All three girls had shown an interest in the handsome young man; to have all three on the same walk must be very flattering for Mr Willoughby. "I'm surprised they have the energy, after all the dancing practice," she said sourly.

Brandon handed over the last peanut to the parrot and sat beside her. "I noticed you didn't appear to be enjoying the dancing."

Jane wrinkled her nose. "Is that a polite way of saying that I was hopeless?"

He shook his head. "It's not your fault if you don't have it in you to dance well."

That was blunt. "Oh, but I'm not usually this bad. I think it is this place." She glanced up at the high ceiling of the gatehouse with its dusty portraits and dim-gold balustrade.

He waited for her to explain. Jane wondered how much she should reveal. Her little trials and tribulations must seem so petty to him, after all he had faced being a slave and a prisoner. He did seem so kind though. She didn't feel he would be a harsh judge.

"You see, Mr Brandon, I do not look back at my time here with any fondness – not like Cassandra. At home, though I am always in her shadow, I don't mind because my family know me and love me in their own way. My brothers think I'm funny, my father encourages my learning, and my mother takes pains to turn me into a young lady. I always know who I am and what I am at home."

He filled the pause with the obvious conclusion. "But not here?"

"No. We came here a few years ago after a very frightening experience at our first school. I was only seven at the time but insisted, or so Mama says, of going with Cassandra when she was sent off to Mrs Cawley's in Oxford. Then an infectious fever broke out and Mrs Cawley moved us to Southampton without even telling our parents. I had no idea what was happening, just that I was bundled into a coach and into a strange building full of sick people – the infection had reached there too." Jane rubbed a scratch on the back of her hand. "It probably travelled with us and we were foolish to try to outrun it."

Brandon cleared his throat, perhaps sensing her remembered

distress. Those weeks still gave her nightmares. "That wasn't your fault. You were only seven."

"Yes, I know. I felt so powerless and I hate feeling that way. Fortunately, one of our friends got a message to her mother and our parents came to the rescue. Not before we all became ill though." Jane nibbled a nail, the bad feelings associated with that time making a ghostlike reappearance. "We were lucky, Cassandra and I. We were nursed back to health. Our friend who had raised the alarm passed the fever on to her mother – and her mother died soon after." Jane had always been haunted by the thought that it could have been her mother, her father, her brothers who could have died as easily from the disease no one could stop.

He swallowed. The conversation had gone into darker territory than either had expected for a story about schoolgirl troubles. "I'm sorry to hear that."

"We all were. I imagine you can see why I was afraid to go off to school again a few months later. Home felt so much safer. Our parents insisted though – they needed the room at home for father's pupils. So we got here and Cassandra loved it – the attention, the praise, being an older girl looked up to by the younger ones, and not just her awkward little sister. She made friends her own age. I'd always tried to be everything to her, but the age gap between us felt bigger than it is now. She could do so much more with the new friends."

"Your sister is almost grown-up?"

Jane nodded. "She is about ready to make her debut in society, to think about courting and young men, maybe even getting married. I will be in the schoolroom for quite a few more years. She needs those friends for the balls and the assemblies I cannot attend. I don't begrudge her the chance."

Brandon was silent for a while, but it was a comfortable pause, as if between friends. "From what you are telling me, it seems that coming to the school feels a threat for you in two ways: it reminds you of a bad time in your life when you were ill and confused without your mother to nurse you, when your life was in danger; and it also is somewhere you feel you might lose your special place in your sister's life."

Put boldly like that, Jane had to admit he was right. "That makes me sound so selfish. Cassandra is the best person in my life. I worry I won't always have her with me. Indeed, I should face the fact that I probably won't."

"Not if you both grow up to get married and have your own families, like most young ladies do," Brandon agreed. "But, Miss Jane, you have her now. I've never seen two sisters who were closer. You should not borrow trouble from the future and spoil the present."

Jane bumped shoulders with him. "Thank you. And you're right, of course. I'm sorry I've told you all this. You must think me very foolish."

"Quite the opposite. And I thank you for your trust. I don't have many friends who confide in me – it hasn't been possible in my life."

"Then please consider me one." Jane felt tears pricking her eyelids. He was such a kind young man and life had been so unfair to him.

Brandon also showed that he was not one to indulge in maudlin thoughts. He stood up. "It is hardly surprising with all this resting on your shoulders that you feel weighed down when dancing. Let me see if I can help you overcome that much at least."

Going with his change of mood, Jane laughed and got to her

feet. She already felt better having admitted it all to someone else. "Are you a miracle worker as well as an excellent musician, Mr Brandon?"

"No, but I have learned how to escape into music so the things that are upsetting me are put down for a while. There have been many times when I couldn't play my flute if I spent too long thinking about my situation."

Jane sobered. He was right. Compared to her little worries about dropping down to a lower place in her sister's estimation, he had so much more to be anxious about. Taken from his family, forced into slavery, and yet he had made himself into a young man of such talent. There was no comparison between their situations. At the very least, she should listen to what his experience had taught him.

"Tell me what you do."

He moved to stand opposite her, like a dancing partner would do. "May I?" He held out his hand. Jane slipped hers in his. He shook it from side to side.

Surprised, she giggled and snatched it back. "What are you doing?"

"Seeing how tense you are. You are twisted up with nerves like wire wool."

"Why, thank you, kind sir, for the compliment."

He grinned. "Shake out your arms and roll your head. It is the way musicians warm up to play."

Jane did as he asked.

"Now close your eyes and listen to the music." He slipped the flute from his pocket and began one of the tunes they had danced to earlier. Jane smiled, enjoying the private concert. He took the flute from his lips. "It's a pretty tune. What does it make you think of?"

Jane closed her eyes again. "I think of country walks with my sister. We know that tune and sing the words to it at the top of our voices when we are in the fields."

His lips quirked into a smile. "Excellent. I thought you liked it when I played it this afternoon. Now this time, I'll hum the tune, and we'll do the first few steps together. Think only of that happy memory – not about the school or people watching you. Think about the place that you can escape to in the music." He tucked the flute in his pocket and took her hand again. "Oh, and don't open your eyes."

He began humming and Jane kept her eyes closed as they moved smoothly through the first steps. She made one stumble but was then so busy concentrating on the memory she didn't even notice that her feet were for once following the steps of the dance. Brandon went a little faster, but she kept up. This was wonderful: she could almost see her and Cassandra striding through the copse behind the rectory, singing the words to the chorus to the rooks in their nests at the summit of the trees. Brandon spun her and her eyes flew open but still she kept on dancing, this time smiling into his friendly face. They got to the end of the measure without another mistake. They dropped hands, panting a little. There was a little moment when something hovered between them, some little sparkle that Jane had never felt before. Then he broke the moment and bowed, and Jane curtseyed.

"Oh my goodness: I didn't know I could do that!" Jane said breathlessly, pressing her palms to hot cheeks. "You must have cast a spell to stop my feet stumbling."

He shook his head. "No, Miss Jane. Music is the spell. You just have to let yourself come under its power and it has the ability to take you away from everything – for a little while at least."

With a final bow, he headed out of the door, closing it quickly behind him to defeat the parrot's escape plan.

Jane picked up a fallen peanut and offered it to Don Pedro. "Now that is what I call a true gentleman," she said, rubbing the parrot on the breast as it clasped the nut in its claw like a jewel of great price. "I'm pleased to report that I'm no longer scared of the ball tonight."

"Beginners please!" commented Don Pedro.

In their little room near Madame's study, Jane and Cassandra helped each other dress for the ball. They could hear the hired musicians tuning their instruments downstairs. One thought of Brandon among them, her newest friend. She had not mentioned the little dancing session to Cassandra but wasn't sure why. It felt too precious somehow; she wanted to cherish the conversation to herself a little longer. Grandison curled up on a rag rug near the empty grate, grumbling mutinously that his wandering had been restricted since late afternoon. Jane had worried for the fate of the supper Madame had gone to such pains to produce.

"You saw her prepare it herself? Why not send out to a bakery to provide the supper for us?" asked Cassandra.

"Money, dear sister, money. Madame is in trouble, or had you not noticed how threadbare the school has become?"

Cassandra laced Jane's stays, not too tight or it would be impossible to dance. "To be honest, I had not."

"No, you've spent your week looking at Mr Willoughby with those great cow eyes of yours."

"Have not!"

"Have too!"

Cassandra shrugged. "Oh, all right, maybe I have looked

at him. But you must agree he is so handsome."

"He insulted me."

"He didn't mean you to hear." Cassandra bit her lip. That had been a definite mark against her favourite.

"I think he didn't care if I did. Anyway, he has no more sense than a newt – and I might be defaming newts by that statement, as I've never tested their intelligence."

"He dances divinely," said Cassandra wistfully.

"So would a newt, given the chance."

"Mr Willoughby is not a newt!"

Jane was quite pleased with herself that she had driven her sister to make such a ridiculous statement. "Is too!" She caught Cassandra's eye and they both burst out into giggles. "So, which of your five dresses," Jane rolled her eyes, "are you going to wear?"

"The ivory muslin with pink trimmings." Cassandra held it against herself. "Or perhaps the polka-dot white with the lace edge? Which do you think?"

"You'll look lovely in both," said Jane, shaking out her gown, gift of Lady Cromwell during her last adventure, notable for its lily pattern.

"Jane!" wailed Cassandra.

"Very well. The ivory. It is newer and will look lovely under the candles."

Satisfied to have been given a plain answer, Cassandra slipped into the gown and turned so Jane could fasten the row of buttons at the back. "You know that none of this will be noticed once Elinor sweeps into the ballroom in her silk?" said Cassandra, holding out her skirts. "She says she will be dressed in a two-tone fabric made by the weaver to a maharajah and that it is blue, but when it catches the light, it looks pink."

"How very confusing."

"And she has a gold sash," added Cassandra.

Jane frowned, struggling with a reluctant button. "Then she'll look like the Hall of Mirrors in Versailles, all flash and glitter."

"Isn't Marie Antoinette so beautiful?" sighed Cassandra. She avidly followed the fashion journals as they described the French queen's latest triumph in excessive dressing. In the rectory they agreed that Marie Antoinette always seemed so much more dashing than Britain's Queen Charlotte, unpatriotic though it might be to say so.

"I didn't mean that as a compliment." Jane tapped Cassandra on the back when she reached the top button. "All done."

"Do you want me to take out your curling papers?"

"Yes, please." Jane sat before the little mirror and watched as her sister unwound her front hair from the curlers. These were made from the stems broken off clay pipes, rolled into the hair surrounded by paper. The curlers had been put in hot an hour ago and her fringe should now have fallen in ringlets to match Cassandra's natural ones.

But, of course, they didn't. They straggled and flopped like eels escaping the fishmonger's pail.

"Oh, why oh why did you get all the beauty?" cried Jane, looking at the disaster in the mirror.

"Why oh why did you get all the wit?" retorted Cassandra.

"Ahah! You admitted it!" Jane jumped up and clapped her hands. "I'll have that in writing, please."

"Oh no." Cassandra backed away. "I only said it to cheer you up. Now sit down and let me finish. I can rescue your hair if you give me half a moment."

Cassandra did indeed rescue the hair and the two Austen

girls stood in front of the mirror, fully dressed, pleased by the result of their labours.

"We might not be the richest girls in the room, but we are undoubtedly the most fun," said Jane. "Let us enjoy our evening." And now she had Brandon's tuition on how to overcome her nerves about dancing, she was even feeling a little hopeful that she might not disgrace herself.

"Hear, hear!" said Cassandra, squeezing her arm. "And to me you are always the most perfect sister in the world."

"I'm your only sister in the world," observed Jane.

Patting Grandison consolingly, the Austens headed downstairs. They were joined by the other girls emerging from their dormitories, compliments were exchanged, and dresses checked over for snags or pins that needed fastening more securely. At the bottom of the stairs, by the door to the ballroom, they were met by Madame. She beamed at them proudly and handed each a little dance card on a ribbon. Jane looked at hers with dread. This was the first one she'd seen, though she knew they were fashionable on the Continent. Why could ladies not just remember with whom they agreed to dance as they did at the assemblies in Steventon? The card looked like a recipe for humiliation if you didn't get any names against any of the dance sets. If rumours had spread that she was not a good partner, she could end the evening with an empty card as a reminder of her failure.

Her tummy flipped over, nerves making her feel a little sick.

"You are all a credit to my school, girls!" Madame said, a tear glistening in the corner of her eye. "I'm so proud, so proud."

"Curtain up!" squawked Don Pedro, and he flew ahead of them into the ballroom.

Chapter 8

The ballroom looked splendid, thought Jane. Madame La Tournelle had done a good job of covering the cracks with garlands, polishing up the tarnished brass fittings so they gleamed, and waxing the floor so slippers slid gracefully across the surface. The chandeliers were lit, the gowns a rainbow, the musicians tuneful as they worked their way through the list of dances Madame had provided.

Madame could congratulate herself on a successful ball.

Jane had to admit that it was humiliating, though, to have to sit out so many of the dances. She didn't think this was because anyone had mentioned her lack of talent, as there were many much better dancers from the school in the same position. Dr Valpy had only brought with him enough boys to act as partners to half the girls so, while the young men were standing up for every set, half of Madame's girls were left as wallflowers, occupying the chairs around the edges. There were some exceptions: Cassandra managed to attract a partner for every dance, and so did Elinor, resplendent in her shifting gown of blue and pink. Jane couldn't decide if she liked the dress or not. It left an impression, but whether it was good was uncertain, somewhat like the colour of the silk. No one, though, could overlook Elinor's diamond jewellery. The diamond mines of Golconda had done her proud. Jane doubted that the princesses in Windsor had better. Men of her parents' acquaintance often went to India to make their fortunes in the East India Company through rather murky business dealings; her father's own sister Phila had made that journey and married richly out there. Elinor's diamonds were proof that the path to India led to riches beyond anything Jane and her parents could aspire. Only her brother Ned, adopted by the noble Knight family as their heir, could hope one day to give his wife and daughters such jewels. The power of the Company appeared unstoppable.

What did Arjun and Deepti think about that? Jane wondered for the first time. As with her thoughts about slavery, she was just beginning to realize what a complicated place the world was. It was much easier to understand the life of her family and neighbours; the far horizons raised questions beyond her experience.

"I wish we were playing cricket," sighed Marianne, slumping into the seat beside her. Marianne's dress was the second finest in the room – a white and pink striped silk that reminded Jane of the candy canes they had at Christmas. She wore a little gold chain with a tear-shaped diamond pendant – still expensive but not as showy as Elinor's.

"Oh, but isn't it thrilling?" said Lucy Palmer, sitting on Jane's other side. She had a hand-me-down from Elinor so was looking very well in a sea-green organza. "I declare I do not mind if I am not asked to dance a single step. I am delighted just to be here, sitting with you both."

At that moment, a young man came and begged the next dance and she glided off on his arm.

"That delight didn't last long," noted Jane.

Marianne smiled indulgently. "Don't mind Lucy. She likes to please everyone."

"I daresay she has little choice in the matter, being an orphan, dependent on your father's charity." Jane felt for the girl's predicament, but she could not persuade herself that Lucy's obligingness came from a good place inside.

The minuet ended and Michael Redfern escorted Elinor to Marianne's side. "One sister safely delivered," he said with a bow.

"Thank you, Mr Redfern," said Marianne graciously, for all the world as if they hadn't first met knocking a cricket ball for six.

A bell rang – the signal for supper. The musicians, Brandon among them, put down their instruments and retired to the kitchen for refreshments. Conversation swelled in the ballroom.

"Thank goodness it's time for grub," said Michael. He rubbed his hands. "Dancing is hungry work."

Elinor waited until he left in search of the food table. "My head is hurting, Marianne. The pins from this tiara are digging in."

Marianne gave the diamond-encrusted hair ornament a tug.

"Ouch!" squeaked Elinor.

"Well, you always say that at every dance we go to and yet, when I remind you how uncomfortable it will be, you always insist you're going to wear it. And I wager your feet hurt too?"

Elinor looked down at the satin tips of her high heels.

"You do not need to claim otherwise. It's no good. I know because I'm your sister and I'm wise to your ways." Marianne got to her feet. "Let's go upstairs and take them off. You can put on a pair of comfortable shoes so you can join in the last part of the ball. We can be back for the next dance and you'll actually enjoy it in slippers rather than heels. Save us some supper, Jane."

Jane fought her way through the crowd to the buffet. Cassandra was there before her on the arm of Mr Willoughby. He was showering flattering remarks on her sister, which Cassandra was drinking in like a lettuce under a watering can spray on a hot day. Leaving her to her flirtation, Jane grabbed a plate and started piling it with food. She bumped into two of Dr Valpy's boys in front of the tower of sandwiches.

"I say, you have quite an appetite," exclaimed Michael, his own plate equally stacked.

"I'm getting some for Marianne and Elinor," said Jane, blushing a little at being caught in the act.

He chuckled. "Good excuse. Would you like to dance the reel with me? I've been saving it for someone who will make it fun as it is my favourite dance."

The moment had arrived. It was on the tip of her tongue to refuse and spare herself the test of dancing, but she reminded herself she liked Michael, and that Brandon had shown her she could dance if she concentrated on the music, so Jane seized her courage and agreed. "It's mine too!" Jane nodded to her dance card. "I'll fill your name in when I've a hand free."

"And Tom here wants to ask you for the promenade, but he's too shy," said Michael, nudging his red-faced friend.

"It would be my pleasure." Jane beamed at him. Two dances – that was more than she had hoped. She could manage that, couldn't she, especially as the boys were almost friends?

Tom cleared his throat. "And do you think Miss Marianne might be persuaded to try the reel with me?"

"I think I can say she would like that very much."

Spirits buoyed by this news, Jane carried her plate back to the Warrens in triumph, including the good news that she and Marianne had secured partners for the two last dances. They quickly demolished the sandwiches. If the school did go under financially, mused Jane, Madame could well make her next career as provider of food to parties.

Plates emptied, dance partners sought out, the musicians returned, and the ball started up again after the supper break. Jane stood with her partner under the chandeliers and waited for the tune to begin.

"Miss Jane, you might need to open your eyes," said Michael, as Jane closed them to work the spell of getting lost in the music.

"Give me a moment," Jane said, trying to remember what Brandon had taught her.

He laughed and seized her hand. With a tug, she joined the dance and had to open her eyes or collide with the rest of the dancers in her set. Happily, the pace of the fast dance did not give her time for doubts and second-guessing of steps. Jane quickly decided that she loved the reel. It was so fast any mistake was swept away by the pace of the dance, long forgotten before embarrassment could strike. She particularly liked the fact that her partner was so much taller than her, which was a rare experience.

As Jane spun around the room, she saw Cassandra was dancing with Mr Willoughby again – a second dance. She could not stand up with him for a third without scandal, so Jane might have to drop a hint that Cassandra shouldn't let him monopolize her time. Cassandra had many sterling qualities, but her weakness was to become a silly goose when admired by a fine young man.

Marianne and Jane swapped partners for the last dance. Her confidence riding high, Jane walked with Tom to their place in the line. It felt good to have overcome her fear of failure on the ballroom floor and to find it wasn't so bad after all. Cassandra was sitting this one out, it would appear, thanks to a hem emergency on Elinor's fragile silk gown. The two older girls exited for some quick repair work up in the bedrooms, leaving two partners having to ask wallflowers for the final dance of the night. Justice had been done. The wallflowers had had more than their fair share of humiliation.

"Have you enjoyed the ball, Mr Thatcher?" Jane asked, thinking she sounded very grown-up with that question.

The stocky batsman grinned as he presented her his hand for the first move. "I have. I enjoy dancing."

And she noticed that for a large lad he was exceptionally light on his feet. Cricket practice had served him well.

She returned to a more normal, teasing tone with him. "Let me into the secret: did you all learn the dances before tonight? I have to admit the standard of dancing has been much higher than I expected."

"If girls can play cricket, then boys can dance." His smile was enigmatic.

The promenade parted them at that moment, giving time for Jane to work out that the boys had been equally anxious that they not disgrace themselves tonight. It wasn't only the girls who had been all atwitter that week ahead of the ball.

They came back together for the final procession around the ballroom, Marianne just behind Jane, Mr Willoughby escorting Madame La Tournelle. The ball hadn't turned out so bad after all, Jane decided.

Miss Jane Austen's Dance Card (with her own notes)

SET	DANCE	NAME OF PARTNER
Set 1	Allemande (stately paced – like bishops walking)	partner?
Set 2	Cotillion (square dance, four couples, complicated!)	partner?
Set 3	Minuet (a dance for couples)	partner?
Set 4	Reel (fast and fun!) – at last!	Michael "Bowler" Redfern
Set 5	Promenade (walking dance – phew!)	Tom "Waistcoat" Thatcher

Then, just as the musicians began the last repeat of the tune, Elinor rushed into the middle of the floor, looking far more animated than Jane had yet seen her.

"My diamonds!" she cried. "Someone has stolen my diamond necklace!"

Diamond Letter – dashed off in haste

My

dearest

brother Henry,

Cassandra and I upheld

the honour of the Austen name

at the ball, dancing until our slippers

wore out. But little did I expect the day to

end with the theft of diamonds from a girl's chamber!

The announcement caused uproar and demands

that the guilty party come forward at once.

But no one claimed the crime and the

girl's father had to be summoned.

He arrived hot foot and

angry. More soon.

Ever yours,

Jane

Chapter 9

After very little sleep, Madame La Tournelle's girls, the boys from Dr Valpy's, and the musicians were summoned to return to the ballroom. Jane thought it a very sorry place the morning after the party. Garlands wilted on the walls. Candles had burned out in their sockets. Crushed flowers dropped from hair grips scattered the floorboards, mixed with some crusts from abandoned sandwiches. Grandison did his best to tidy up the latter, but even he couldn't improve the general air of gloom.

Mr Warren, Elinor and Marianne's father, stood on the dais that had been erected for the musicians. A wan-faced Elinor drooped in a chair at his side, Madame hovering over her, ready with smelling salts and handkerchiefs. Marianne stood by the wall next to her brother, Edward, who, though he hadn't been a guest, had come to show his support for his sisters.

"I feel like a criminal already," Jane whispered to Cassandra as they were lined up for Mr Warren's inspection.

Once the last person had entered, Mr Warren cleared his throat. Tall, blue-eyed, and blonde, medals on his chest, he looked like the very model of an East India Company officer.

"Young ladies and gentlemen, I have gathered you all here today for a very serious matter. You will all be aware that stealing items of the value we are considering here is a capital offence. If the perpetrator does not admit their guilt immediately, later identification will lead to gaol and a death sentence."

Jane looked down at her feet. Grandison licked her ankle, cheering her a little. She, of course, knew she was innocent, but this meeting was making her feel tarred with the same brush as the thief, no matter how illogical that was.

"If you took the diamonds as some childish prank to annoy my daughter," continued Mr Warren, "then now is the moment to step forward. Your courage in admitting your guilt will lessen the punishment. It will be treated as a matter for school discipline and not for the laws of this land."

A deathly silence fell. No one spoke.

"I see. In that case, I must pursue this as an investigation into a crime of the most serious nature. I will alert the local magistrate and call in one of the Bow Street Runners from London to conduct an enquiry. But first we must collect evidence while it is still fresh. My first question: who knew where the diamonds were kept?"

He directed this question to Madame La Tournelle.

"Oh, oh!" The lady flapped like a flag worried by the wind. "I did not know, that I can assure you, sir, or I would have offered to lock them away in my strong box."

"Elinor?" Mr Warren asked.

Elinor got to her feet shakily. Lucy Palmer rushed forward to support her elbow. "You sent them on Wednesday, Father, as you will remember. I had them taken up to my room. The diamonds stayed there behind a locked door until I wore them at the ball. I returned them to their case during the supper interval." She wrung her hands. "I suppose anyone who saw me leave and return without them at supper might have guessed that I had put them back in their casket?"

"But not everyone here knew where your room was." Mr Warren scanned the room, looking for the telltale flush of guilt or hung head.

Elinor looked panicked. "All the girls did, naturally."

"Anyone else?"

"The boy!" Madame La Tournelle pointed a finger at Brandon. "That boy – I asked him to take the trunk upstairs."

Brandon looked shocked to be so singled out. "Me? But I was playing all evening, up there on the stage. Everyone saw me."

Jane clutched Cassandra's arm. She could feel the way the room was turning hostile against her new friend and she really didn't like it.

"But not during supper, I take it?" said Mr Warren, nostrils flaring like a hound on a scent. "What is the boy's name?"

There was an awkward pause.

"Brandon King. He's my servant. I've always found him a most honest boy," said Mr Willoughby, but his sideways look at his flautist undermined his spoken pledge of good character. The other musicians edged away from Brandon, not wanting to be tainted by suspicion.

"He carried up the casket, but did he know about the diamonds before the ball?" asked Mr Warren.

Elinor nodded. "Yes, sir. I did mention them. Is that not so, Marianne?"

Marianne bit her lip. "You did, but there were others present – Mr Willoughby, Madame La Tournelle, and some of the girls."

She glanced at Jane as if appealing for help.

"I hope you are not suggesting *I* took them?" said Mr Willoughby with a great show of hurt. "I am a gentleman!"

Marianne had not suggested that, but Jane now began to wonder. The dancing master certainly could do with the money.

"Well, it seems we have our first suspect," said Mr Warren. "We must detain the boy and search him and his belongings. You boys!" He clicked his fingers at two of the older students from Mr Valpy's school. "Arrest the African."

And that was why Mr Warren felt able to take such a daring step – because Brandon was an outsider, of a race many of Mr Warren's type assumed were inferior! Jane's anger swelled at the injustice. She quivered with rage. Only yesterday Brandon had stopped out of the kindness of his heart to help a girl overcome her fear and learn to enjoy escaping into music; surely he was not the kind of person who would steal from another?

"Jane!" whispered Cassandra, feeling the explosion building beside her.

"You can't do that!" Jane declared, pushing to the front of the girls. "There's no evidence to lay against him!"

"And who are *you*?" thundered Mr Warren, looking down on the thirteen-year-old girl who dared to challenge him. Girls were clearly another inferior species as far as he was concerned.

"I am Miss Jane Austen of Steventon Rectory and friend to Brandon King." Brandon shot her a surprised look. From the tension in his frame, braced as if for a blow, he had clearly been expecting the whole room to turn against him. "You cannot go throwing accusations around just because you do not respect Brandon!"

"That has nothing to do with it!" fumed Mr Warren.

"Hasn't it? I also saw the jewel casket, as did my elder sister, your niece Lucy, the headmistress, and the dancing master. Why are you not arresting all of us?"

"Maybe I should!"

Jane threw up her hands. "There is clearly no reasoning with you." Why were adults so prejudiced?

Just then, making use of her distraction, Brandon bolted for the door. A boy grabbed for his jacket but he slipped out of it, wriggling free, leaving the empty garment behind. Grandison bounded after him, thinking this all a frightfully good game, tripping many of the pursuers in the process. The front door of the Abbey gatehouse banged open, Don Pedro squawked, and Brandon fled.

"Oh dear," muttered Jane, gaze stuck on the jacket hanging in a boy's fist. That did not look good. But she could hardly blame him for taking his chance.

"Do you still think him innocent?" sneered Mr Warren. "Raise the watch! Ten-pound reward for the person who captures the boy."

That sowed confusion in the ballroom as Dr Valpy's boys all streamed after Brandon without waiting for permission from their teacher. It was like the parrot hunt again but without the good humour.

Jane caught Tom and Michael as they hurried past. "He's not guilty," she said. She was following her gut instinct that he was innocent, as at this stage no one could know for certain what was true. This was certainly no way to conduct an investigation: shouted accusations and a manhunt!

"Let go, Miss. Better we find him than the others," said Michael, giving her a sympathetic look. He darted for the door.

"Don't worry, Miss Jane, we'll make sure we bring him back unharmed," promised Tom, then he too ran for the street.

Chapter 10

What a disaster! Jane sat at the edge of the stage in the empty ballroom, petting Grandison. The girls had followed the search party outside and could be seen gathered in little groups on the green, speculating as to how long it would take the boys to find Brandon. Jane hoped the search would meet with as much success as the most recent attempt to retrieve the parrot.

Cassandra returned from outdoors and sat down beside her sister.

"Why do you think Brandon ran, Jane, if he is innocent? Would it not have been better to stay and argue his case?"

Grandison turned his brown eyes to Jane, eyebrow hairs twitching as if to second the question.

"I've been thinking about that," said Jane. "From what he told me, Brandon's experience of people has been terrible. He was taken as a slave, then press-ganged and not allowed ashore for years, so he can be forgiven for running before someone has a chance to fetter him again."

"But if there was no evidence, he would be let go."

In Jane's opinion, Cassandra had too strong a belief in the rational behaviour of mankind.

"What reason does he have to trust that? Mr Warren was quick to believe in his guilt; would he not be equally quick to make up a story about passing the diamonds off to accomplices?"

Cassandra kicked the hem of her dress moodily. "It's not fair."

"I would think Brandon might claim those words as the motto of his life so far. But we can't sit by and let this injustice happen. We should help him." Jane stood up, decision made.

"I agree, but how?" Cassandra got up to stand beside her, backing her as she usually did, even when she wasn't sure of Jane's wisdom.

"I see two things we can do. Get Brandon to safety and find out who really stole the jewels."

"How can we do that?"

Jane paced, working out the details of her idea. "I think... no, that's no good... yes, that might work."

Cassandra tapped her arm. "What might work?"

"The thing I'm thinking of."

Cassandra sighed. "You really are the most infuriating person to be sister to sometimes."

Jane grinned fiercely, her appetite to see justice done stirred. "I know – but you still love me. Let's go."

Cassandra tied her bonnet back on. "Where?"

"To find Brandon, of course." Jane clipped a lead to Grandison's collar.

"How do we get to him first? He has half of Reading looking for him and they've got a head start on us."

"But half of Reading doesn't have Grandison." Jane kneeled and held her dog by the nose so he knew she was serious.

"Grandison, find Brandon." She offered him the jacket that had been dropped as Brandon dashed from the room. She let him sniff and snuffle the pockets. "Find this boy."

Grandison wagged his tail and Jane took that as agreement. "Lead on, good dog."

Grandison put his nose to the ground and did as requested.

Grandison's nose took them in a circle out to the street then back into the school.

"I think he's lost the scent already," said Cassandra, shading her eyes against the sunshine as it poured through the trees in the Abbey gardens.

Jane noted how Grandison's ears were pricked. He did not show any signs of confusion. "No, I think our quarry was being clever. Brandon is clearly very intelligent, so we should think like a wily boy who is used to running." Grandison trotted through the archway and out into the school grounds where so far he had been forbidden to roam. "The Abbey ruins make a splendid place to hide."

Checking they were not being followed, Jane let Grandison pull her over toward the tumbled walls of what was left of the old Abbey complex. Some of the walls had archways and niches set in them. He stopped by one of these, built some eight feet up, and barked.

Don Pedro poked his head out of a little niche.

"It's just the parrot, you silly dog," said Cassandra.

The bird took flight but Grandison did not chase. He remained, nose pointing upward. Jane thought his attention was on an even bigger hole further up.

Quickly looking around to check no one was in sight, Jane called up: "Brandon? It's me, Jane. I'm with my sister – no one else."

No reply.

"Cassandra, can you go to the end of the path and warn us if anyone approaches?" said Jane, loud enough so that Brandon would hear.

"Yes, of course. Brandon, we really do only want to help," said Cassandra, before heading off to keep watch.

"Look, I know you have no reason to trust me but I want to help you." Jane waited. "I know you're hiding up there – or at least Grandison does."

There was the slightest scraping of feet over rock and Brandon appeared, lying flat on his belly, to look down at her.

"Thank you," said Jane, taking that as a declaration of trust. "Your idea is a good one. They won't look for you here when they think you're hiding somewhere in the town, or on the roads out. Stay there for now and I will sort out a place for you to stay. We'll move you under cover of dark – agreed?"

"Yes," he whispered.

"If we can slip away without being seen, we'll return with some water and something to eat. For the moment, remain where you are and try not to worry."

"Who will take me in?" asked Brandon. "I'm a wanted man."

"You are a wrongly accused boy," said Jane, "and I have some very reliable people in mind."

Cassandra called from the end of the path. "Jane!"

"Must go." Jane threw up the jacket so he at least wouldn't get cold. "I'll be back soon." Then aloud she added, "Coming, Cassandra. Grandison is such a naughty dog to slip into the garden without us noticing." She tugged him along with her, hoping he would stop looking back at where Brandon was hiding.

Joining Cassandra, she saw what had caused her sister to call out. Madame was bringing tea to Elinor, Marianne, Edward, and their father on the garden terrace. There was cake, so Grandison dragged her in that direction.

"I told you not to let that dog into the garden!" scolded Madame as soon as she saw them approach.

Jane tried to look sorry. "I apologize. There was so much commotion outside that he chose the quiet of the garden for his —"

"Yes, enough said, I think." Madame turned to Mr Warren. "Miss Jane Austen here is only a visitor to the school. You mustn't judge my girls by her behaviour."

"Very irregular — bringing dogs into a school for ladies," huffed Mr Warren.

"I like Grandison," said Marianne. "He's a wonderful fielder."

"A what?" Mr Warren turned to his younger daughter, probably wondering how she knew such things.

"A young lord at my old college had a bear," offered Edward. "We all thought him a first-rate chap."

Marianne's brother has mastered the art of the well-timed distraction, thought Jane with approval.

"A bear? That's ridiculous!" spluttered Mr Warren.

"Not at all. He rescued him from a street entertainer who had mistreated poor Bruno. After a few weeks, the novelty of sharing a bedroom with a bear wore thin and he packed Bruno off to his estate, where I understand the bear is living in happy retirement." Edward held out his cup. "Any more tea where that came from?" Madame poured from a great height, much to the young man's approbation. "Thank you. Chasing about town is thirsty work."

"You haven't found Brandon then?" asked Jane innocently.

"No, and I suppose that pleases you?" said Mr Warren.

"Aren't you the one who spoke up for him?"

"I did, but only because I felt it was unfair to single him out on no evidence. You see, crimes need three things: motive, opportunity, and means."

"You, a girl, wish to lecture me on this, do you?" Mr Warren gave her a sour smile.

Jane chose to ignore his sarcasm. "Thank you for asking my opinion. The way I see it, Brandon's motive is no greater than anyone else's – his opportunity was the same as the others who attended the ball – but means? That's the really interesting part. How did he get up two flights of stairs to the girls' dormitories and pick a lock without being spotted? Elinor cannot have been the only person who went back to her room during supper to mend her dress or change her slippers. He could not have done it later because he was playing. Yet no one said they saw him on the stairs or lurking around up there. You see, he really is not a very good suspect."

Elinor placed a hand on her father's arm. "Oh, Father, maybe we have accused the wrong boy? He was only doing me a service carrying my trunk upstairs, and this is how we repay him."

"And why was he doing that in the first place?" asked Mr Warren, scowling. "Most irregular."

"My manservants are on holiday – unwell," said Madame, inventing wildly. "I am woefully short-handed at the moment."

Mr Warren turned his frown on her. "Which is it – holidaying or unwell?'

"They were unwell so went on holiday." Madame was blushing so disguised it with a flutter of her handkerchief.

"Both of them," said Mr Warren evenly.

"It was very infectious, I understand."

Mr Warren looked at her with displeasure. "I think I had better take my daughters home with me."

"Oh no," said Marianne quickly. "I like it here. There's so much to do." Her eyes went to the archway leading to Forbury Green. Jane could tell she was thinking of the unfinished cricket match.

"But it is clearly not safe," her father said in a tone that was meant to be final.

"Father, I feel I am somewhat to blame for the incident with the diamonds," Elinor said humbly.

Yes! thought Jane.

"My dear, you mustn't feel guilty for wanting to wear your mother's jewels." Mr Warren patted her hand.

"But I could, as Madame said, have entrusted them to a more secure place. I would like to stay here at least until we get them back or find the perpetrator. Perhaps we can then decide if this school suits both Marianne and me?"

"I'm happy here. I like being near Edward," put in Marianne.

Mr Warren ignored her. "You are right, Elinor. We should take this one step at a time." He looked at his pocket watch. "Thank you for the tea, Madame. I must go. The Bow Street Runner I hired is due on the afternoon coach from London."

Madame left with him to show him to the door.

Jane took a vacated seat and helped Grandison to a biscuit to thank him for his triumph of scent following. "You know, Elinor, to prove that Brandon did not take the diamonds, we really do need to find out who did. Did you see anyone when you came down from your room last night – anyone on the stairs?"

Elinor wrinkled her brow in thought. "Only Lucy. She was talking to Mr Willoughby in the passageway leading to the kitchens. I think she followed me back into the ballroom though, as I later saw her at supper with some of the other girls."

But Lucy was a poor relation, relying on the charity of the Warrens. She had a strong motive to try to get some of the family wealth for herself, and she would have known where the diamonds were kept.

"Was the casket locked?" asked Jane.

Elinor looked down, shamefaced. "I'm afraid not. I was in a hurry so I put the diamond necklace on the top layer with the tiara. I thought the locked door would protect them. Only the necklace was gone when I went back."

"That is something we haven't yet considered: why take just the necklace? If you were going to steal one item, why not all of them?" asked Cassandra.

"Perhaps the thief only had a pocket to hide something in quickly so dared not be greedy," suggested Marianne.

"Or he didn't have long so just grabbed the first thing he could?" said Edward.

"And did you close and lock the door when you left?" enquired Jane.

"I did," said Elinor.

"And it was closed and locked when you returned?"

"It was. Cassandra was with me so will remember I had to unlock it."

Jane thought back to the sultry summer night. "Was the window open?"

"Yes, but we are on the second floor. Do you think someone could climb up?"

"I was thinking more that they might have climbed down. The Abbey gatehouse roof can be reached by the staircases on either side. Let yourself down on a rope a few feet, no one would see you."

"Are you thinking a professional burglar might have done it?" asked Edward.

Jane chewed a fingernail. "It is possible – and there is one at work in Reading according to the reward notices that have been posted – but then why leave the rest? That doesn't seem the action of a competent thief."

"It certainly is a mystery," said Cassandra.

"Good thing I like solving them then," said Jane. "Any tea left in that pot?"

Chapter 11

The moon was rising above the gatehouse when Jane crept out. She had made a passable mound in the bed to fool Matron's late-night checks that she was inside, and Cassandra had promised to cover for her if necessary. Hardest to persuade to stay was Grandison – he always liked a good adventure – but they had managed this by Cassandra holding his collar as Jane slipped out. They had to hope he didn't start howling, but had secured a supply of stale biscuits to pacify him just in case.

There was plenty of light from the full moon so Jane went without a lantern. She crept into the Abbey ruins and called softly for Brandon. A thump on the grass told her he had heard and jumped down from his refuge.

"All quiet," she assured him.

"I've left the jug and plate in my hiding place," he told her. Cassandra had taken some supplies out earlier in the evening.

"I'll return them tomorrow. Let's get you away now."

"I can't thank you enough for helping." He moved much more quietly than her, Jane noticed. She looked down and saw that he had removed his boots. Good thinking, but too late for her.

"No need for thanks. You should not be in a position where you needed help. This is about getting you justice."

The archway was closed by two heavy wooden gates that looked like Abbey relics, but Jane had already taken the key from its hook inside. This was a splendid piece of metalwork with a bow like an oyster shell and stars cut into the ward, the end that clicked with the lock. Sliding it into the big lock, she puffed and strained as she moved the heavy mechanism.

I should have oiled the hinges, she thought, as one side swung open with a creak.

A flickering light went on in one of the windows. Someone had lit a candle in Madame's study.

"Quickly now," she whispered.

Pulling the gate to, but not closing it fully so that Jane could get back in, the two fugitives ran down the road toward the market square. Jane expected the hue and cry to sound at any moment but the night remained quiet.

Once around the corner, they slowed to a walk. Few people were about, but there were some late-night travellers outside the inn and farmers' carts heading to the markets in London.

I should have brought Grandison after all, thought Jane. No one would think twice about two people walking a dog.

"Where are we going?" asked Brandon in a low voice.

"Somewhere they won't think to look. You'll like it." Jane knocked on the door of the bakery. The bolts slid back inside. "Special delivery," she announced to Deepti.

The baker's daughter shook her head in warning and beckoned them in, taking a careful look at all the buildings surrounding theirs to see if anyone was curious. The door closed behind them.

"You really should not talk when on a secret mission," said

Deepti, taking Jane's cloak and bonnet from her.

"Deepti, you'll remember Brandon, from the cricket match." The flautist bowed. "Brandon, you can trust her. She's a trained bodyguard so knows how to look after people."

"Jane exaggerates. My father is the one who is the trained bodyguard; I am merely learning a few things from him," said Deepti modestly.

"Don't believe her. She is quite the most accomplished girl in swordplay and archery that I have ever met. That really beats ladies painting screens and doing embroidery, in my estimation." Arjun had indeed trained his daughter, as in their culture rich ladies often had female bodyguards.

Brandon looked bemused by the girls' chatter. Taking pity on his confusion, Deepti beckoned him to follow her.

"Please, come and see my father." She led them into the bakery where Arjun was kneading bread for the first bake of the morning. The room had a lovely warm, yeasty smell. It was hard to believe anything bad could happen in the world when standing in the middle of a bakery.

"It is rather late for you, is it not, Miss Jane?" Arjun said, holding up floury hands in a wave of greeting.

"Late but necessary. Thank you so much for agreeing to hide Brandon. Hopefully it will only be for a few days until the real culprit is found." Jane peeked in the bowl and saw a mound of pale dough rising like a plump chest heaving in a sigh.

"It is our pleasure to help you, Brandon." Arjun nodded to a stool. "Sit down, young man, and we'll give you a late supper. Jane mentioned that you would not have eaten."

"Thank you, sir." Brandon took the stool indicated. "I am much obliged. But I do not want to just sit back while others go about saving me; I want to do something to prove my innocence."

Jane sympathized with him. In his shoes, she would feel the same. It was infuriating to rely on others. "Unfortunately, I don't believe a disguise would work in your case. Perhaps if you take over Deepti's duties here at the bakery, she would then be free to ask some questions on your behalf?"

Brandon thought for a moment and gave a reluctant nod. "I would be grateful if she did and I want to make myself useful."

"Of course, I will. But what kind of questions?" asked Deepti, taking a plate that had been warming on the stove and putting a generous serving of rice and stew in front of Brandon.

Jane took a chair opposite Brandon. His supper looked much better than hers had been, a golden curry with crisp bread to go with it. "I think we should find out more about those diamonds," said Jane. "Mr Warren acted as if the only suspects could be those at the ball, but others in his household would know about them. How many of them knew where they were sent, and had time to plan a burglary while we were all distracted?"

"Mr Warren, you say?" Arjun frowned. "I remember him from home. Was he not the Collector in Hyderabad?"

"What is a collector?" asked Brandon.

"The person in charge of collecting the taxes paid by the local population to the East India Company. We pay for the pleasure of having an army in occupation," said Arjun with a sour smile.

Brandon nodded. "Ah yes, extortion. I understand."

This was not the explanation Jane had heard at home. "But I thought the army was required to help maintain the peace in the Indian kingdoms?"

"And who do you think is wanting to disturb the peace? Could it be the local people who do not want a foreign company taking all their money?" suggested Arjun.

"Oh." Jane did not like to feel stupid. Put that way, the system did seem wrong. Even in her little corner of Hampshire, she saw many injustices committed by the powerful. Landowners were enclosing the common pastures for their own use, pushing out the local people and their flocks. Was that so different from the empire builders who were closing up countries to others who might want to trade? They were enforcing it, not with a fence, but with guns. She would have to think about this further, Jane decided. For the moment she needed to work out the relevance to her case. "Then you think Mr Warren is truly a very rich man, even if his wealth comes from unworthy sources?"

Arjun dusted off his hands and put the dough in a warm place to rise further. "He should be if he is like other senior officials, but why is he not still in Hyderabad?"

"I believe he is delivering his girls to an English school now they are old enough to leave him."

"But why not send the daughters back with a female chaperone, as other officers would have done?"

Jane thought it very useful to have someone used to the Indian end of this mystery. She wouldn't have thought to question this. "Do his actions strike you as unusual?"

"That depends. It may coincide with a period of home leave due to him," said Arjun.

"He does have a son here whom he has not seen for a few years," offered Jane.

"Another possible explanation. I am only remarking that usually the man in charge of the nest of the golden goose rarely leaves it untended for the months that this Warren is spending away from his post. Greed and self-interest would forbid that."

Deepti had been listening to all this very carefully. "I know:

I will take a basket of our cardamon cakes to his kitchen tomorrow, pretending to be seeking new customers. Hopefully, they will ask me in while they taste them and I can listen in to the gossip in the servants' quarters. The servants usually know more about what is going on than the masters."

"Thank you. That would be very helpful." Jane wrapped her shawl around her shoulders and picked up her bonnet by the strings. "I'd better get back before I am missed."

Arjun took off his apron. "And I insist on escorting you. The streets after dark are no place for a young lady to walk alone. Brandon, my daughter will show you your room while I am gone. We also have a cellar where you can retreat should anyone come looking – she'll show you that too."

"Thank you, sir." Brandon stood up and bowed.

Arjun wrapped a dark cloak over his white baker's clothes. "Say nothing of it. Just return the favour to another unfortunate when you have the chance in the future."

With that, Arjun escorted Jane out and back through the silent streets to school.

A No I-dea Letter

My dear Henry,

The absence of the jewels becomes more and more troublesome for Cassandra and me. When we rose Saturday morn, we looked hard at the bedroom from whence the gems were taken and we found matters very hard to decode. The top layer of the casket was empty, but many treasures lay beneath that were not grabbed by our burglar – brooch, hand adornments, coronet, gemstones for ears – all these were present. Only the necklace was gone. Cassandra and her pal (me) searched the room for clues. The casement was open because that fatal eve was hot and sultry, but how anyone could clamber up or down was beyond our powers to deduce. We went to the roof to check and could see no safe passage, and thought only a cat could manage such a feat. Was the felon someone from the Abbey School perhaps? we wondered. Hard to prove unless we uncover the necklace on the wrongdoer's person.

Before that moment comes, poor Brandon, the flute player, suffers under false charges and has been forced to conceal where he has taken cover from those that hunt for that unfortunate boy.

Yet the gems stay lost and your females here have no explanatory theory. The costly stones are gone – just as one letter of the alphabet has departed from the page thanks to my careful management of words.

Have you found out my playful jest?

Yours ever,

Jane

Chapter 12

"Do you want to return home?" Cassandra asked when Jane got back from posting her letter to Henry. Agitated, Cassandra smoothed down the quilt on their bed and plumped the pillows. "We were only invited until the ball and that is now well and truly over. We could stay one more night and leave tomorrow."

"I don't see how we could." Jane sat down on the window seat, relishing the warmth of the afternoon sun on her arms. Below she could see a gaggle of girls playing catch in the Abbey gardens, carefree, not acting as if someone's life was at stake. "As much as I enjoy the prospect of returning home, we now have a certain person relying on us." She glanced meaningfully toward the door.

"You think someone might be listening?" mouthed Cassandra.

Jane nodded.

"Who?"

Jane spelled out the name. On her return, she had caught Lucy Palmer skulking in the passageway. Lucy had the look of a girl who made a habit of listening in doorways – that and flirting with dancing masters. Jane changed the subject, speaking loudly. "Have you quite got over your infatuation with Mr Willoughby, oh sister mine?"

"I am not infatuated!" protested Cassandra.

"You cannot fool me. You were more than a little taken with him. At the ball, you danced twice with him – and you know what that means." Jane wiggled her eyebrows.

"It means we enjoy each other as a dance partner." Cassandra smirked.

"Fiddlesticks. It is a clear mark of favour. You were both billing and cooing like the squire's doves." Jane dropped her voice to a more confidential tone. "Does he know that you are but a rector's daughter with no promise of more than a tiny dowry?"

"Jane, it is not like you to go from two dances at a ball to imagining I have made plans to wed." Cassandra slumped down on the bed she had just tidied, rumpling the covers again. She stretched her arms above her head. "I'm too young to have such thoughts. There are many years of dancing and beaux before me."

"That is the first rational thing I've heard you say on the subject for months. Good, because now I can tell you that I suspect Mr Willoughby might have had a hand in the theft."

Cassandra threw a cushion at her sister. "Take that back."

"Very well." Jane threw the cushion at Cassandra. "There: you can have it back."

"I meant about Willoughby."

"*Mr* Willoughby," said Jane, a little alarmed that despite her words her sister had lapsed into such a familiar form of address.

"That's what I meant. You should not accuse him simply because you do not like him."

"Am I the kind of girl to make baseless accusations? I'm not like Madame La Tournelle or Mr Warren. Also, these are not accusations but theories. If you cannot hear me out, then I will find someone better to talk to – like Madame's parrot!" Jane got up, pretending to leave.

Cassandra pulled a sour face. "Oh, very well then. I apologize for overreacting."

Jane sat back down. "I understand, Cassie: you like him. But how much do you really know about him?"

Cassandra propped herself against the headboard and hugged the cushion. "He's a dancing master. He rebelled against his father to follow his chosen profession."

"Yes. I know that too – as does all the world."

"He says he is twenty-five."

"So old!"

"He adores music. He knows all the latest tunes from London."

"Naturally."

Cassandra produced her trump card. "And he did offer a position to Brandon in his household. He took a risk when he took him off the streets. That must indicate a generous nature."

"That is a decided mark in his favour. Weighed against this, though, was his failure to protest Brandon's innocence more vigorously when he was accused yesterday."

Cassandra wrinkled her brow. "I have to admit that was not Mr Willoughby's finest hour."

"Yes, his finest hours come in the ballroom. I fear there is little to admire outside it."

"Now you are being harsh again!"

"Harsh but truthful, I fear."

"Then tell me: why do you suspect him?" Cassandra played with the cushion tassel, forcing herself to listen even though she would much prefer to remain with her illusions about the handsome dancing master.

Jane counted off the reasons on her fingers. "He was there when the diamonds first arrived so knew where they were. He was seen in the passageway during the supper break so conceivably could have run upstairs. A teacher is far less likely to be questioned than Brandon. He was able to leave after the ball and thus dispose of what he took, unlike most of us. He is poor and desperately in need of funds – as witnessed by his threadbare clothes."

Cassandra was not yet ready to give up his character. "I'm sure he is a very respectable young man."

"He looks respectable, but it is the respectability of a man who is only just clinging on."

"Poverty does not make you a thief," countered Cassandra.

"Of course not, but it does make the temptation all the greater. He could have reasoned that Elinor has no need of those diamonds, not with all the other jewels in her casket. She won't even miss them long, as her father can replace them easily, thanks to his wealth. Just slip them in a pocket, dash off home, and hope no one thinks to look too closely at you when they decide who might be to blame. He might even have calculated that they would suspect Brandon before him: the foreigner versus the native-born gentleman."

"You make him sound a scoundrel. I do not like it." Cassandra slid off the bed and straightened her skirt. "Are you coming down to dinner?"

Jane rose to her feet. "I'm not saying it happened this way; I'm merely sketching out one plot for how things happened that night."

"You look at people with a jaundiced eye sometimes, Jane."

"I look at people with a satirical eye all the time, Cassandra: I thought you knew."

At dinner with the other girls, Jane looked down the table, going from face to face, trying to decide if anyone was showing signs of guilt or even satisfaction to have got away with so audacious a theft. Under the dusty chandeliers of the largest room in the school, apart from the ballroom, the pupils were gossiping about the necklace theft, speculating as to when Brandon – the supposed burglar – would be found. They had been questioned by Mr Warren's Bow Street Runner investigator, and a number of them claimed to have suspected Brandon from the start on the grounds that he had stared at Elinor's necklace all evening. Jane had noticed no such thing; from what she remembered, he had been looking at his music. For all the chatter, malicious though some of it was, she concluded either the pupils were all very good actresses or they were as they appeared: empty-headed and innocent.

Giving up on her watery soup, Jane paid special attention to Lucy Palmer, sitting with Elinor and Marianne at a table apart. She was consoling Elinor as usual, smiling sweetly at Marianne whenever she could. *It must be exhausting to make yourself pleasant all day*, thought Jane. The Warrens were served superior rations to everyone else, fresh butter on the table and white bread, rather than the coarse stuff the others had to consume, so that was reason enough for Lucy to worm her way into their good graces.

Jane then turned to the head of the pupils' table. There was a new occupant in the chair reserved for the headteacher. Madame herself was absent, dining with the investigator and

Mr Warren, leaving the job of overseeing the diners to Matron.

What about Matron? She was another who could move freely about the school without being questioned, but thus far Jane had not had many dealings with her. Matron – or Miss Brown to give her true name – was a very small person, no more than four and a half feet tall, so that Jane felt a giant beside her and thus did not elect to stand in her vicinity. Someone was bound to mock. Matron's once fair hair was turning a premature wispy white, her dress a dove grey, serviceable and darned in places, her cap starched but in need of fresh trimming. She had not been at the school when Jane and Cassandra had attended, but it had not taken them long on this visit to realize that the girls were not scared of her. Matron's discipline was more due to the fact that nobody wanted to upset her.

"Cassandra?" Jane whispered. "What do you know about Matron?"

Cassandra dipped her stale crust of bread in her soup, hoping to soften it so it would not pain her jaw when chewing. "Lucy told me that Matron is a niece of Madame – that she grew up in Madame's house."

"How does Lucy know that?"

"As you've already brought to my attention, Lucy has a habit of ferreting out facts about people – rather like you."

"You did not just compare me to Lucy Palmer!" Jane was tempted to upend her soup into her sister's lap for that insult.

"Not the motives, but you must admit you both spend your time puzzling out what other people are up to."

"But I don't listen at doors – at least, not often." Jane wasn't sure if she should continue a line of questioning when the information Cassandra had would have been gathered in an underhand manner. In the end, she decided Brandon deserved that she bend her rules a little on his behalf. "And where did they grow up?"

"In London, apparently. Lucy says she heard Matron refer to Madame by her first name of Sarah. Is that a French name?"

"I dare say you will find French girls called that as it is from the Bible, but none of us actually think Madame is French, do we?"

"I suppose not," Cassandra conceded.

"Matron's accent is pure London from what I've heard. Perhaps we should look for Madame's origins there too?"

At that point Don Pedro fluttered into the dining room and landed on their table. The girls all gathered their bowls closer, not because he would want to eat their human food, but because he had been known to put his beak in it as an experiment.

An experiment in what? Jane wondered. Annoying them, probably. He appeared to regard the school as a venue for mutual torment.

He strutted down the table until he came to stand in front of Jane. Her heart beat a little faster. There was something savage about the bird for all his exuberant plumage. He cocked his head. His white beak had a cruel black tip on the end, and his wings were fringed with yellow and blue feathers, like a Spanish shawl.

"*¡Hola!*" said Jane tentatively.

He tipped his head the other way.

"I don't think he is really Spanish," said Cassandra.

"I do know that, Cassie. I was being satirical. You do realize that he's named after a character in *Gulliver's Travels*, don't you?" Jane wished he would move on. "Did you know that parrots can live for fifty years or more? He could be a very old parrot by now, alive during the reign of our king's grandfather."

"How do you know that?" Cassandra offered the bird a crust from her plate, which he ignored.

"Father's library. He has a book about birds."

"I do declare, Jane, you spend more time in Father's library than he does."

"If he did not insist on having it to himself when writing his sermons in there, I would!"

Just then, Don Pedro bobbed up and down and croaked at the top of his voice: "Curtain up!"

The girls within earshot giggled. He bobbed forward again, very pleased with himself. This time he opened his beak to fasten it around the end of a little egg spoon, flapped, and took off. He flew out the door into the corridor.

Suspicions roused, Jane leaped up.

"Follow that bird, Cassandra!"

Cassandra dropped her spoon. "What?"

"That bird. We follow. Now!"

"But I haven't finished eating!"

Jane ran out of the hall, even though girls were forbidden to leave the table until given permission. With a sigh, Cassandra abandoned her meal and set off after her. All eyes turned to the Austen sisters running from the room.

"Girls!" squeaked Matron. "Girls!"

"Sorry, Matron!" Cassandra called. "Jane has had to leave suddenly. I must see if she is all right." Cassandra did not like to lie, but she was at peace with letting her hearer draw the wrong conclusion about a sudden bout of sickness.

Jane had followed Don Pedro into the high-ceilinged gateway. He had taken the teaspoon up to a window at the very top, reachable only with wings or a very long ladder, but onward flight was impeded by the glass. From what Jane could see from the ground, the only things up there with him were dead flies and a huge spider's web. He glared down at the girls.

"Beginners please!" he hooted at them. "Beginners, beginners, beginners, pur-lease!"

"Jane!" said Cassandra, catching up with her sister. "What on earth are you doing? That's not even your teaspoon. Why are you chasing him?"

Jane stood with her hands on her hips, not taking her eyes off the bird. "Cassandra, I think I know who stole the necklace."

Cassandra followed her gaze upwards. "Don Pedro?"

"Don't you remember, the window in Elinor and Marianne's bedroom was open? He is the only one who could have flown in. Sparkly jewels – that's just what this bird loves. One grab with his beak and he could flap away, no one the wiser."

"He's our burglar?"

"That is what I believe. What we've got to work out now is, where would he hide it?"

Chapter 18

That night, Jane and Cassandra were out of bed again, this time searching for parrot hideaways in the Abbey gardens.

"We are going to get caught!" Cassandra moaned. She was less happy than her sister creeping around the school with a candle. The Bow Street Runner, who had introduced himself as Mr Jennings, had been lurking around the school all day, looking for his own clues. Everywhere they had turned, every corner, every classroom, he had been there before them, a distinct tall, thin man with a head as bald as an egg.

"Mr Jennings went to his inn at nine. I watched him go," said Jane. She had to pretend the confidence her sister so clearly lacked, like a captain leading his troops into battle. "We won't get caught."

"You say that and then we always get caught."

"Only because you panic and make too much noise. Mama is a light sleeper." At home in Steventon, Jane had noticed that Cassandra lacked the qualities that made Jane a good spy. It was probably because Cassandra's looks meant that too many people paid attention to her, whereas Jane was good at slipping away to get on with the things she preferred to do, like reading and writing in a quiet corner.

"I can't help it – I'm nervous." Cassandra was shivering even though it was a warm night.

Jane stopped, put her candle down, turned, and gave her sister a hug. "Be brave, Bold Cassandra, the Austen pride depends on you."

"That is what I'm afraid of – that I'll let you down."

"Concentrate on what we have to accomplish. Brandon needs us to do what he cannot at the moment. I find that helps me when I'm feeling scared." Jane looked up at the walls, pierced with lots of parrot-sized nooks and crannies. With a little imagination, you could add the roof, the painted walls, the statues, and stained glass and transport yourself back to the time when monks, rather than schoolgirls, studied here. "I think we can eliminate the place where Brandon hid. He was in there for a long time so he would have noticed."

"Agreed." Cassandra sounded relieved.

"I'm going to climb up to that hole there, where we saw Don Pedro." She pointed. "You hold me steady so I don't fall down."

"Be careful!"

Jane drew her petticoat up through her legs to tuck into her waistband, creating an approximation of baggy bloomers. "I wish I could borrow Henry's clothes for this. Why are our brothers allowed much more sensible clothes in which to have adventures?"

"I believe that is rather the idea behind ladies' clothes – they force us to be ladylike."

Jane snorted and wedged her boot tip in one crack while she reached up with her left arm to wiggle her fingers into a chink. "Boost me up."

Aided by her sister braced behind her, Jane groped around in the hole. Her hands fastened on something hard and smooth. She grabbed it and dropped back down.

"Let's see," said Cassandra excitedly, holding up her candle. Jane opened her hand.

"A rock," said Jane. "I suppose it was too much to hope that we would strike lucky on the first attempt."

"Not just a rock." Cassandra turned it over. "Look: it's the head of an angel. It must have broken off a statue and tumbled in there."

"When wicked King Henry dissolved the monasteries." Jane clutched the angel head to her chest. "Poor old angel."

"Let's keep looking. Where next?"

"To the next hole. Lead on, sister mine."

Ten holes later, the girls gave up their search for the night. Their candles had burned down to stubs, and Jane's fingers were aching and scratched from all the digging she had been doing in the debris left by centuries of neglect. They had found nothing as rewarding as the angel's head after their first foray, and Jane had had to paw her way through rather too much disgusting grime left by pigeons and rotting leaves. A thorough clean of her hands was the first item on her agenda when they got back to their chamber.

Traipsing back to the gatehouse, Jane remarked, "You know, Cassandra, the other place we saw Don Pedro was out on the Forbury. In fact, I should have thought of that first, for it is easier to fly from Elinor's bedroom to that big oak tree."

"Would a necklace still be there?" asked Cassandra. "Boys climb those trees. The parrot might even have dropped it as it flew. I doubt very much a passer-by would think twice of pocketing a chance-found diamond necklace. They are probably in London selling it for a hundred pounds even as we speak. You could live for years off what that would fetch."

Jane had to allow that Cassandra was right. "That would be a grievous blow to our plans of proving Brandon's innocence. But we have to look, don't we?"

"We do, but I do not think we can get away with climbing the tree in full view of both this school and Dr Valpy's windows."

"I agree," said Jane.

"And I don't want to risk leaving school grounds again after dark like you did last night."

"I also agree. We need daylight for our search."

Cassandra heaved a sigh of relief.

"Which is why I thought we would recruit Michael Redfern and Tom Thatcher," continued Jane. "No one would think twice seeing them shin up and look."

The next morning they could not immediately embark on their plan because everyone was expected to attend morning worship at church. Jane and Cassandra went with Madame's delegation to sit in their allotted pews. The boys were tantalizingly close, but there was a sea of respectable grown-ups in the pews between, the two schools positioned on purpose to keep boys and girls apart. Jane sat in a pool of sunlight, finding that warmth helped her think.

How to alert Michael and Tom that they are needed? wondered Jane. Inspiration struck as she admired the coloured reflections on the floor, cast by the sunlight pouring through the stained-glass windows of robed saints and harp-playing angels. She dug in her little pocket that hung on a string from her waist. Her oldest brother, James, had given her a small mirror in a seashell case for Christmas one year. It was useful for reading mirror writing, another of their little family games. She flipped it open, slid it across her skirt for where the sunlight fell on her knees, and searched for the right angle. The reflection danced on the ceiling but slowly she lowered it.

Cassandra, realizing what Jane was doing, picked up her hymnal and held it so Madame, seated at the end of the pew, would not see Jane's lap.

A little lower... a bit more... Yes! Jane grinned as the reflection hit the side of Michael's face. He batted it away, confusing the reflection in his eye with a fly landing on him. Catching the flash across the nave, Tom was quicker to grasp what was going on. He elbowed Michael and nodded across the church to Jane. Jane held up two fingers, hoping they would understand that they were to meet at two o'clock on the green.

Michael frowned.

Apparently not.

Jane glared.

At that point, rescue came in the form of the vicar announcing the next hymn. In the distraction of people finding their place, Jane mouthed: "The Forbury. At two."

Michael nodded, then his eyes widened and went to the person at the end of Jane's pew who had turned to look at him.

"Miss Jane," said Madame, looking across at Dr Valpy's boys, then leaning around Elinor, "it seems your attention is wandering. Have you lost your place? We are singing hymn fifty-six, not making eyes at boys across the church."

"Thank you, Madame," said Jane meekly while slipping the mirror back in her pocket. "It's one of my favourites."

"Raised in a rectory indeed!" Madame muttered.

Raised in a rectory to stand up for what is right, thought Jane. She and her Maker were on very good terms as to the relative importance of paying heed to the sermon and saving a boy's life.

A Reflection on Our Situation

My dear Henry,

Just a quick note dashed off when I heard a messenger was heading your way. Having settled on a chief suspect – Madame's thieving parrot – we hunted high and low. Our search within the Abbey proved fruitless, so we recruited two boys from the neighbouring school to climb Don Pedro's favourite tree. Our hopes were raised when they returned with several teaspoons and an old bangle. Delving deeper, though, the necklace was nowhere to be found.

Were we right to suspect the parrot? It certainly explains the mysterious ability of the thief to pass unseen. Or were we accusing an innocent bird?

None of this matters, as we cannot prove the theory either way. I am quite despondent that we will not be able to help our friend. Perhaps we should think of a way of getting him out of Reading and away to safety?

Your affectionately,

Jane

(See p. 171 to read the letter from left to right.)

Chapter 14

With the excuse that she was taking Grandison for his walk, Jane slipped out of school and headed for the bakery. Her mind was busy sifting through the things she had learned, very much like a baker sifting his flour to break up the lumps impeding his work. After the disappointment of finding that Don Pedro had not hidden the necklace in the tree – or if he had, it had been taken – she was left with more questions than answers. Her reading informed her that there were several species of birds that liked to steal shiny objects, magpies most famously, but she had never heard this of a parrot. How had the bird picked up this odd behaviour?

The streets were quiet this late on a Sunday afternoon, shadows lengthening under the trees of the Forbury and on the High Street. All shops were closed; only the inns showed signs of life as travellers broke their journey to and from London in the many hostelries that served this trade. It was a relatively easy day's ride from here to the city. Had the necklace already gone that way?

She tripped. Looking down, Jane noticed that her bootlace

had come loose so she stopped to tie it. Grandison nosed in the gutter, then along a brick wall, marking the places where his rivals had paused. Above him flapped posters advertising plays, concerts, and other performances for the townsfolk. A circus with wild animals had set up on the meadow by the Thames to the north of the city. Perhaps Madame La Tournelle would be proved wrong and elephants would walk the local streets? mused Jane. If the worst came to the worst, would they send Brandon away with it? Circus folk were known for living outside the usual rules and his musical skill would be welcome.

"What do you think?" she asked her dog, but Grandison had other things on his mind.

Jane moved on, tugging Grandison away from a favourite tree. When they reached the bakery, the shutters were down so she went around the back and knocked on the kitchen door.

After a few seconds, Arjun opened it only a crack. "Miss Jane, we were wondering when we would see you." Opening it more fully, he glanced around to see if she was being watched. "Come through: we are in the kitchen. Deepti is out at the house we mentioned." That meant Deepti was taking cakes to the Warrens' servants. "You've news, I hope?"

Brandon was sitting at the kitchen table, decorating some pies with sprigs of thyme. He looked up and smiled as she came in, though the worry lines did not completely go from his brow.

"I have news, but it is not completely good, I'm afraid." And she told Arjun and Brandon about Don Pedro and the possibility that the parrot had dropped the necklace outside the school, so that it would never be traced again.

Brandon looked grim. "If someone picked it up, then I am doomed. Everyone will blame me."

Jane squeezed his hand. "Don't give up hope, Brandon. We

are better fishers after the truth than that. We've still got many lines we can tug. Also, I was wondering if we should approach the circus people and see if they will take you in? That will be a good place to run to, if Arjun and Deepti cannot hide you any longer. No one looks very closely at circus folk, because their eyes are on the far more exciting sight of the lions and elephants."

"A circus?" Brandon looked puzzled. "What would I do there?"

"You could hide – but, in time, once you are far from here, your music will always be welcome and earn your keep until you find a safe place to remain."

He nodded, accepting the plan. "Please, ask if they will harbour me."

"You will approach them?" said Arjun sceptically. "You, Miss Jane Austen of Steventon Rectory?"

He was right. Jane might think of herself as very capable, but she was just a thirteen-year-old girl in a darned muslin dress and bonnet; such a delicate question would come better from a more impressive grown-up. "Will you come with me, Mr Arjun?"

"With pleasure." He unfastened his apron. "I was merely waiting for you to ask." He hung the apron on a peg. "I for one have always loved a circus."

"We'll leave Grandison with you," said Jane, handing the leash to Brandon. "He will keep you company and you can keep him out of trouble."

Brandon sighed, inactivity clearly not suiting him. "Come on, boy," he said to Grandison, "let us go to my room."

The circus was quiet on this Sunday afternoon. No public

performances were allowed on the sabbath, which gave the circus people time to set up and enjoy a day without visitors swarming through their encampment. Jane could see their gaily striped tents and coloured wagons from a distance. Pennants rippled from the top of the flagpoles. *Where are their animals?* she wondered. The posters had promised an elephant, a lion tamer, and trick riding. Looking more closely, she now saw a couple of heavier, larger wagons with bars, home to the unfortunate big cats who had to spend their lives imprisoned. The horses were more fortunate: they were in a corral near the water's edge. *Oh and yes!* There was the elephant, down by the river. Then Jane noticed, in the creature's shadow, a man in a white loincloth standing in the shallows, scrubbing the grey-brown flanks with a brush. She had often had to wash Grandison after he had got muddy; this looked a much bigger and more satisfying task. At least the elephant did not look likely to shake dirty water over you when you finished.

"Who is that, do you think?" Jane asked. "An elephant keeper?"

"A mahout," said Arjun.

"A what?" Jane got out her notebook, excited to find a new word.

"The word for a trainer of elephants in India. It is an honourable profession."

Jane decided that if she couldn't be a bodyguard like Deepti when she grew up, then another dream job would be a mahout. Any Austen, with the possible exception of her mother and Cassandra, would jump at the chance to wash an elephant. Sadly, that was likely to remain just a dream, as there were few elephants to be seen in Hampshire. She put her notebook away. "Shall we approach?"

"If he signals that it is safe. Elephants must be respected," said Arjun seriously.

Jane was more than ready to offer the elephant all the respect she would show a visiting duchess. Cautiously, they drew near to the riverbank. They weren't the only locals to be watching the unaccustomed sight of an elephant bathing in the Thames. Several families had brought picnics and set up on the other side of the river, the children screaming with delight when the beast squirted water with its trunk.

Arjun raised his hand and began speaking rapidly in his native tongue to the mahout. The man turned in surprise on hearing a compatriot address him. The mahout called out a greeting. What followed was a rapid exchange, laughter, and much head shaking. Jane guessed they were lamenting the oddity of the English people they lived among who thought elephants unusual.

The mahout gave his charge a final scrub and led it out of the river. Jane marvelled at the sad patience of the beast. Then she noticed that an iron chain ran between its front legs, hampering its stride.

"Does it have to be chained?" she whispered to Arjun, not wanting to offend the mahout.

"Betty might wander if she were free and this is better than a cage," said the mahout, revealing he had both good English and excellent hearing. "She is fond of buns and has been known to go in search of them at night to the detriment of the supply wagon."

"You called your elephant 'Betty'?" Jane was incensed on behalf of the majestic creature.

"She has had to become an English elephant, never to return home, so she needed an English name. I was told Betty sounded friendly. Was that not right?"

"I suppose it is," Jane conceded. She dipped a curtsey. "Jane Austen, at your service."

He bowed. "Sanjay, at yours."

"It is a piece of luck finding another Indian person here," said Jane, looking to Arjun. "Have you mentioned our friend?"

Arjun smiled, amused by her tendency to rush ahead, Jane suspected. "Not yet. May we talk to you for a moment, Sanjay?"

Sanjay began leading Betty toward her pen. "I have many moments to spare if you do not mind sharing them with us both. Come along." It was not clear if he was talking to them or Betty. Maybe all three.

As the two men talked, Jane watched Betty make her way through a heap of hay, lifting trunkfuls to her mouth and chewing thoughtfully. Her little dark eyes appeared to be as interested in Jane as Jane was in the elephant – until, that is, the trunk made an exploratory journey toward Jane's new straw bonnet and ruffled the brim. Sanjay gave a bark of a command and Betty turned back to her hay with only the smallest sign of disappointment.

There were worse fates for a bonnet, mused Jane, tweaking hers back in place, than to become dessert for an elephant.

After a few more minutes of conversation, Arjun stood and shook hands with Sanjay.

"You've agreed?" asked Jane eagerly, brushing straw from her skirt. A trunk snaked over and helped in clean-up. "Thank you, Betty." She told herself not to be scared, but it was hard when the trunk in question belonged to so big a creature.

"Yes. Our friend will hide here and leave with the circus if we cannot prove his innocence," said Arjun. He rubbed the back of his neck. "I have to say, that is a load off my mind."

"Is your friend fond of animals?" asked Sanjay, scratching

Betty behind her flapping ear, a gesture she seemed to enjoy immensely, "because I am in need of a helper."

"Well, he likes Grandison and he is quite a big dog," said Jane thoughtfully.

"We will ask," said Arjun. "Until later then?"

With a few more words of parting, Jane and Arjun left Sanjay and Betty to enjoy the rest of their sunny afternoon.

Most satisfactory, thought Jane, and what a letter she now had to write home.

A Letter of Elephantine Importance

To my dearest
Henry. Today I
had the great
pleasure of pay-
ing a call on an
elephant called
Betty. She sends
you her regards. In
other news, Deepti
has made friends
at the Warrens' house
and discovered all is not
as well as Mr Warren tries
to pretend. He had quickly to
leave his post under a cloud.
The nature of the scandal is yet
to be discovered, but I must truncate
my letter here because my trunk is complete.
Yours affectionately, Jane.

Chapter 15

Once alone in their bedroom, the two sisters began to get ready for bed. It was one of Jane's favourite times of day, when she had her sister to herself and they could exchange the news they had gathered. Normally this was the little doings of the people of Steventon, but today they had much bigger things to discuss – in the literal sense of that word.

Cassandra was very jealous when she heard that Jane had spent the afternoon with an elephant.

"You always go on the most splendid adventures without me," she complained as she unbuttoned Jane's gown for her. "This has to stop."

"Really?" Jane contemplated her bonnet, pulling at the frayed edge; it had not stood up well to Betty's interest. She decided she would have to donate it to the elephant next time they met. It was now no use for anything else.

"Yes." Cassandra huffed over a particularly troublesome button.

Spinning her poor bonnet in her hands, Jane smiled. "Then next time come with me."

"One of us had to stay and keep an eye on the Bow Street Runner in case he came back." Cassandra tapped Jane's back to signal that she was done.

"Any more sign of activity from him?" Jane wriggled out of her dress, swapping it for her nightgown.

"Yes!" said Cassandra eagerly. "I was so distracted by your tales of elephants that I forgot to tell you. Mr Jennings climbed the tree! It was most entertaining as it took him a few goes, and I think he might have split his breeches in the attempt. I watched him from Elinor and Marianne's window."

Jane paused in the middle of fastening the ties on her nightgown. "What? He climbed the oak Don Pedro perches in?"

"Exactly. That is not a coincidence."

Jane sucked on her bottom lip. "No, it is not. He must've been spying on us this afternoon," she said, half to herself. "I wish he wasn't so thorough in his job. It is making ours far more difficult. When was this?"

"About half an hour after you left with Grandison." Cassandra turned back the sheets and got into her side of the bed.

"Good, so he didn't follow me." At least Brandon was still safe where he was. However, an efficient Bow Street Runner meant they might have to move him earlier than they had planned. Jane had an itching along her spine that something was amiss. Though she was a rational girl, she also trusted instincts. She went to the window. Was that Mr Jennings out there even now, waiting to see if either girl slipped out to go to the fugitive? As Jane watched, two figures appeared and met on the street below, cloaked and hatted – a man and a young woman. The woman slipped her arm through the man's and they hurried off. It was too dark to see who they were, but Jane did not think the man was short enough for the Runner. He was rather tall and held himself well. Perhaps it was merely a lovers' meeting? A maid who had sneaked out to see her beau?

"Tell me more about what Deepti found out," said Cassandra, punching the lumpy pillow in the hope it would be more comfortable after a pummelling.

Jane turned away from the window and drew the curtains. "I fear Marianne and Elinor's father is in trouble."

"Do tell me more." Cassandra, eyes bright with interest in the candlelight, looked like a squirrel in a white bower ready to crack the nut of news.

"Arjun noticed that it was unusual for an East India Company official to leave his post for so long, especially one as valuable as that which Mr Warren holds."

"Go on." Cassandra patted Jane's side of the bed. "But don't you dare put your cold toes on me."

Jane got into bed and rubbed her feet to warm them up. Even in summer the bedrooms in the school were chilly. "The servants said that there were complaints made against Mr Warren that he had been keeping some of the money meant to pay for the army and instead used it for his own expenses."

"Expenses such as draping two daughters in diamonds?"

"He claimed those were gifts from a maharajah, but in essence you are correct. Marianne and Elinor have been raised like princesses. The money for that has to come from somewhere."

Cassandra gathered her hair to one side in a bunch. "So it is not the amount he is taking from the Indian people that is disputed – it is how much he is passing on to other British officers?"

"Correct. But the situation gets even more interesting, according to Deepti." Jane curled her knees to her chest.

"His defence against the accusations, which he put around in Hyderabad, is that he isn't as rich as people think – and his servants tend to agree. They've not had a pay rise for years."

"He could just be a miser," suggested Cassandra.

"True, but why choose Madame's school for his girls? He does not stint when it comes to Elinor, and this place is hardly the byword in girls' education for fashionable families. Most pupils are like us – well-to-do but not rich."

Cassandra made a humming noise as she pondered this, plaiting her hair to fit under her bed cap. "That is odd, I grant you."

Grandison put his nose hopefully on Jane's forearm, but she pointed him firmly to his blanket on the floor. He settled down with a woof. "You are going to grant me more when I remind you that Marianne said it was Elinor's choice to come here. From what I've seen of Elinor, she would prefer to be somewhere where she can impress everyone with her diamonds. As much as I like Reading, the town is sadly provincial, the society somewhat limited."

"But their brother…?" began Cassandra.

"Marianne is close to him, not Elinor. And that only since they came here – they barely knew him before. The school was already decided upon without that being a factor in its favour."

Cassandra finished tying her night braid. "You are clearly thinking something, Jane, but I do not see it yet."

"I'm thinking that it is true that the Warrens might not be as rich as they appear and Elinor knows it. She is helping out her father by pretending this is her choice. Even if they have lost half their wealth, she will still be a notable heiress by Reading standards. There would be more scrutiny in London or Bath where the highest in society are found."

"I see." Blowing out the candle, Cassandra burrowed down into the bed. "I think that makes me like her more. Perhaps her air of superiority is an act to hide the fact that she knows they are on a sticky wicket?"

Jane giggled at her sister's cricket metaphor. "Indeed. We really need to finish that game. Marianne will never forgive us if we don't."

The girls were woken at six the next morning by a commotion in the passageway. Madame was screaming, and even Matron had raised her voice above a soft whisper and could be heard calling upon the heavens to help them. Jane threw the covers aside.

"Come on: something has happened."

Rather more blearily, Cassandra slid her feet into her shoes. "What now?"

"Let's find out." Grabbing a blanket to wear as a shawl, Jane added, "I'm so glad I persuaded you to come for the ball – this is so much more interesting than home!"

She hurried out into the corridor before Cassandra could throw a pillow at her. As soon as the door opened, Grandison shot ahead. He joined the knot of girls who were huddled in distress and added his comforting barks to the throng. Jane made a beeline for Marianne, who was standing a little apart, hand resting on Elinor's shoulder as the elder sister sobbed.

"Oh, my poor school!" wailed Madame. "This will be the end of us!" In her white nightdress and robe, with a huge lace cap, she collapsed into noisy sobs, resembling an undercooked meringue sagging flat when removed too soon from the oven. She had to be led away by Matron.

"Not another theft?" asked Jane. She had rather supposed

Mr Warren would've removed the remaining diamonds immediately after the first.

"No, but some*one* has stolen away," said Marianne. "Lucy, our cousin, left in the night with Mr Willoughby."

"What – they've eloped?" Jane shook her head in disbelief. That made no sense. Mr Willoughby had shown little favour to Lucy Palmer; his attention had all been on Elinor, the heiress, and Cassandra, the beauty. What had she missed? Then Jane thought of the meeting during the ball supper break and the shadowy figures outside she'd seen from the window last night. She hadn't been taking notice of who had been flirting with whom, but it was possible Lucy had been conducting a clandestine romance under all their noses. She had outsmarted them all.

"I'm afraid it is true," said Elinor, mopping her cheeks with her wrist. "She left me a note."

"May I see?" Jane asked.

Elinor nodded and handed it over.

My dear Elinor,

I'm sure you will think it the merriest news ever when I tell you where I am gone, and I cannot help laughing myself when I imagine the faces of everyone tomorrow morning when they find my room empty. I am off to Gretna Green – but can you guess with whom? I will forgive you if you do not get it right on first attempt, for I know we have hidden our attachment from all eyes.

Do you want to know with whom I have run away? I will give you a clue: I hope my next letter to you will be signed Lucy Willoughby! Yes – Mr Willoughby is the one. I love him even more than I love to see him dancing. We will both be as happy as can be together as soon as we are wed. We hope to call on you on our return from Scotland as man and wife. Give my love to Marianne and my duty to your father.

Yours affectionately,

Lucy

Jane passed the letter to Cassandra.

"What a note to write at such a time!" said Cassandra. "And such a serious step to undertake in so light a frame of mind!"

Jane suspected that the lightness was a pretence. There was more to scheming Lucy Palmer than a frivolous girl who risked her respectable status in society by running off at seventeen to marry a dancing master. "What is in it for him, I wonder?" she mused aloud. Lucy she could understand: to be married so young and taken out of living a life of humiliating dependence on her relatives was a prize any impoverished girl might find tempting. Plus, Mr Willoughby was handsome, had begun his own business, and was a very fine dancer. But what did he see in Lucy? She was pretty enough but had displayed no obvious accomplishments, unless determination and sneakiness could be counted. "She has no money?"

"No, none at all," said Elinor. "Though my father had

promised to find her a dowry in a year or two when his finances allowed."

But if Lucy knew that the Warrens' wealth was an illusion, perhaps she had decided to bolt with the first likely gentleman before news got out in England that the Indian coffers were bare? That made more sense to Jane than any other explanation. Lucy might have suspected that things were coming to a crisis for the Warrens and knew she had to leave now before she went down with that ship.

"Will anyone go after them?" asked Cassandra, her thoughts still on the fate of the couple rather than on the reasons behind the reckless elopement.

Marianne shook her head. "I doubt it. My father is more concerned about finding the diamond necklace than chasing across England after a relative on our mother's side. I'm afraid Lucy is quite lost to us."

Elinor stood up and tucked her handkerchief away, showing the steel in her character that she had hidden so far. "Indeed. Lucy has made her choice and must now live with it. I hope they will be happy, but we cannot ruin our own chances of a respectable marriage by condoning her actions. I'm afraid Lucy is no longer to be received at our house."

It was a sad truth, thought Jane, that society punished those who broke the rules and ran away to get married, rather than wait for their parents' approval. It was a herd instinct, parents fearing if they let one girl get away with it, they would start a stampede of their own offspring marrying imprudently for love.

"But Lucy had no father to give permission," said Cassandra. She was always more soft-hearted than Jane. "Surely she can be forgiven in time?"

Elinor tugged her shawl close, a gesture that spoke of

someone wrapping herself up against scandal. "But our father was her guardian. If she had asked him, I doubt he would have refused her if she told him that she truly loved Mr Willoughby and he her. Mr Willoughby has a profession, if not a good income. Father is not an unreasonable man."

That cast a new light on the subject: why run if permission had not been denied and would likely have been given? A new idea blossomed in Jane's mind. Were the couple hiding something, like the fact that they relied on a stolen item to fund their new life? That would buy them a dancing studio in London or another city at the very least.

"Marianne, how good would you say that Lucy is at climbing trees?" asked Jane.

Marianne looked thoughtful, catching on to Jane's suspicion. "I'm not sure, but I do know she has a talent for knowing what is going on."

"I still think someone should go after them," Cassandra said plaintively.

"Don't worry, Cassie. I have a feeling they might be back very soon of their own accord," said Jane.

Chapter 16

Later that morning Jane received a note from Deepti. Arjun and Deepti had decided they had better take Brandon to his new hiding place at the circus at first light. While running errands, Deepti had seen Mr Jennings walking up and down the road outside the bakery – that could have just been a coincidence, but they had agreed not to underestimate the persistent Bow Street Runner. An early morning visit by the miller with sacks of flour had given the baker and his daughter the perfect way to smuggle Brandon out. Brandon had emerged from the journey at the circus unharmed but looking like the ghost of Hamlet's father, according to Sanjay.

Jane showed Cassandra the note.

"I don't like the way we keeping moving Brandon about as if he were no more than lumber to be put into storage," fretted Jane. "I think we should make sure he is happy with this new hiding place."

"True. But how do you suggest we get out unobserved?" asked Cassandra, setting the note on fire and dropping it into the fireplace to destroy it.

"You are right." Jane frowned at herself in the mirror, catching her sister's worried gaze in the reflection. "We've got to be more careful. That dratted Bow Street Runner seems to be turning up everywhere."

Cassandra wiped the ash off her hands with a washcloth. "I think I've an idea. Leave it to me."

When Cassandra suggested that she and Jane escort some of the younger girls to the meadows, Madame La Tournelle was delighted – and unsuspicious. Preoccupied with trying to save her school by hiding the double disaster of a girl *and* diamonds missing from her care, she had little to time to consider summer treats for her charges.

"Thank you, Miss Austen, I can always rely on you," Madame said pointedly to Cassandra, not looking at Jane. "The younger girls will love that. Nothing like a country walk to cheer one up in the face of adversity."

Jane didn't think the younger girls were feeling any of the adversity experienced by Madame La Tournelle, but she wasn't going to argue when the Austen sisters had got their way.

Hearing that an outing was on offer, the younger girls swarmed into the gatehouse. Jane began to wonder if Cassandra's plan was so good after all. They would have their hands full making sure they returned the same number as they took out.

Cassandra and Jane were marshalling their flock in the gatehouse, tying bonnet strings for the youngest, when Mr Jennings sidled up.

"Miss Austen?" He tipped his hat to Cassandra. "Miss Jane Austen." He touched his brim to Jane. "I've been wanting a word."

The sisters exchanged a look. They had been rather pleased

that they had managed to avoid questioning so far. The excuse that they weren't pupils at the school had allowed them to duck out every time he tried to summon his witnesses to give their version of the events surrounding the burglary. It seemed that there was no more ducking to be done.

"I'm afraid we are just on the way out," said Cassandra, succeeding in making it sound as if she was sorry. "We are looking after the younger girls this morning."

"Then perhaps I can escort you?" he offered gallantly, "and ask my questions as we walk?"

The last thing they wanted was to lead him to Brandon's new hiding place.

"Oh, I think we might have a few moments to spare," said Jane breezily. "Girls, would you take Grandison to the Forbury? We'll be along shortly."

The most responsible of the younger girls took hold of the dog's lead and led her party out. The noise level rapidly descended from deafening to bearable.

"How may we help you?" asked Cassandra once they could hear themselves speak.

The Runner sized them up, dark eyes intelligent but not sufficiently awake, Jane thought, to the capacity of his audience. Used to dealing with London's hardened criminals, he probably thought two young ladies from a country rectory no challenge. "You are the last two witnesses who were present on the night of the ball still to give me your testimony as to what you saw."

"I'm sure we saw much the same as everyone else," said Jane quickly. "I was dancing the last two dances." She tried to look like a silly girl with only dancing on her mind.

"And I accompanied Miss Warren to her room and was with

her when she discovered the loss," said Cassandra. "I saw what she saw – an open casket, an open window, no necklace."

Mr Jennings nodded and took out a little notebook from his pocket. "And why did you go to the young lady's room, Miss Austen? Your own room is not in that corridor, I believe?"

Cassandra took the question with its note of accusation in her stride. "Miss Warren had ripped a hem. I was going to do a quick stitch to stop the tear getting worse."

"She's very good at quick stitches," Jane added helpfully.

Mr Jennings nodded as if that corresponded with what he had already noted. He licked the tip of his pencil and made a jotting. Jane was fascinated how his shaven head shone dully in the light forcing its way through the dusty windows of the gatehouse. Most men either wore a wig or powdered their hair. Her own father had a good head of curls, and all her brothers were too young to have lost theirs. This Runner had decided a hat was sufficient to cover his pate. Tall and thin, Mr Jennings reminded Jane of the knob-handled walking stick used by the old man who often sat by the village cross in Steventon. The head of that too had been worn to a shine from being gripped in gnarled fingers.

"Miss Jane, you first came to my attention when you made a vehement defence of the young African. May I ask on what grounds you exonerated him?" asked Mr Jennings.

"On the grounds that there was no evidence, only prejudice against him," said Jane stoutly.

"We are all innocent until proven guilty, are we not, sir?" said Cassandra, in a friendlier tone.

"That is very true, young miss, but it does not help prove that innocence if you make a run for it. There has been a thief at work in Reading for a few weeks now, a period that matches the

time when the boy first entered service with Mr Willoughby."
Mr Jennings turned a page in his notebook. "So you haven't
seen the boy since?"

"Which boy?" asked Cassandra, not wanting to lie.

"The boy suspected of the theft, of course."

That let Cassandra answer with full honesty. "No, we have
not." Neither of them suspected Brandon of the deed. "Are you
looking at anyone else in relation to the matter?"

"I was curious," Mr Jennings said carefully, "why you asked
two boys from the other school to climb the oak tree opposite
the window."

There seemed little to be lost in admitting the truth. "We
were investigating a theory about the theft," said Jane.

The Runner turned back to her. "Which was?"

"Madame La Tournelle's parrot steals things – shiny things
like silver spoons and hair grips. We wondered if it had flown
in and taken the diamond necklace."

"Through the open window? Hmm, interesting." He made a
note.

"Why did you climb the tree?" asked Cassandra. "I saw you
do it yesterday."

He didn't look pleased to have been spotted. "I thought you
had a different idea," he said reluctantly.

"Which was?" asked Cassandra sweetly.

"That someone had thrown the necklace out of the window
to an accomplice, and they had hidden the necklace there so it
would not be found on their person."

That was a very respectable theory. Jane was impressed.

"But it seems we were both wrong," Jane said. "The necklace
wasn't there."

"Wasn't there *any longer*," he said with emphasis. "But the cavity in the tree was sufficient to stash a necklace. This is a well-practised operation we are dealing with – work of more than one pair of nimble fingers. I don't think the boy had time to return for it when we chased him from the school ballroom, but perhaps his accomplice did?"

Jane's moment of being impressed passed swiftly. "No, because Brandon doesn't have an accomplice. He is innocent."

The Runner gave her a look that said she knew nothing of the world. "We shall see."

"Yes, we shall. Now is that everything, Mr Jennings?" Jane adopted the chilly tone her mother used to get rid of visitors who stayed too long.

"For the moment."

Jane gave him a nod, one investigator to another. He might not realize they were in competition, but in her mind they surely were. "Then we will get on with our programme of events."

He turned to go. "Oh, I meant to ask: where are you taking the girls?"

"For a treat," said Cassandra airily. "A walk in the meadows."

"A botanical walk. We'll be collecting useful plants," said Jane, worried he would take it into his head to follow them. "Would you like to carry this for us?" She held out an empty basket she had been planning to fill with buns for Betty.

The Runner looked worried that he might find himself spending his valuable time scurrying around behind a flock of flower-picking girls. "No, thank you, delightful though the offer is. Some of us have work to do." His smile was humourless.

"Good day, sir," said Cassandra.

Once on the street, Jane sighed. "Drat. I suppose we have to pick some leaves now and impart what little botanical knowledge we have to the girls."

Cassandra laughed and linked arms with her. "Don't worry, Jane. I for one have been paying attention to Mother's lectures in the still room."

"I do too."

"No, you do not. You only perk up on mention of poisons."

Jane smiled and elbowed her sister. "Well, you never know when you might need them, being an Austen."

Jane left Cassandra and Grandison with the party of girls by the riverbank and slipped away to look for Brandon. She found him in Sanjay's caravan. This was a delightfully painted wagon with a canvas roof, decorated with lotus flowers and Indian creatures such as tigers, elephants, and snakes. Brandon himself was lying on a bunk, reading. She tapped on the door, the top half already open to let in some air.

"Brandon, how do you like your new accommodation?" Jane asked.

He sat up cross-legged, looking much happier than when Jane last saw him. And was that a little flour still dusting his hair? "It suits me well. Please, come in. This wagon reminds me of the captain's cabin on board my old ship. Would you like some tea?"

Getting up gracefully, he poured her a little cup of fragrant liquid from a kettle sitting on a tiny stove. Jane laughed – it was like being in a doll's house.

"It is like a miniature – I love miniatures. They capture the spirit of a person or place perfectly, better than many a larger canvas." She sat opposite him on the other bunk.

Brandon poured himself a cup. "I'm pleased you came to visit, Miss Jane, because I have been doing some investigating of my own."

"Really? Oh good: what have you found out?" asked Jane.

"I've been thinking about the parrot and what you said about his odd habits."

"Go on."

He made her wait as he took a sip, then he put his tea down. He leaned forward, getting down to business. "Coming here made me wonder if it were possible to train a creature to do something like that against its natural instincts. So I asked around the circus because I thought they would know."

From the twinkle in his eyes, Jane could tell he had something to tell her but was enjoying sharing it at his own pace. "And did they?"

"Apparently there once was a famous circus act at the Haymarket in London. Do you know it?" He fluttered his fingers in the general direction of the capital, some forty miles to the east.

"Yes, a theatre in London. It is well known for its sensational shows."

"The lion tamer remembers a double act of two Cockney women who had some marvellous trained animals – the Hackitt Sisters. One of those was, or so he thinks, a parrot who would take items from members of the audience and carry them to the stage. They also had trick ponies and a troupe of dancing dogs." Having presented his news, Brandon sat back and folded his arms in satisfaction.

Jane tried not to get distracted imagining Grandison dancing. "I don't suppose the lion tamer remembers the name of the ladies – or the parrot, come to that?"

"No, but he says he recalls what they look like. Perhaps he can describe them to you?"

Jane drained her teacup. "Take me to the lions, please."

Chapter 17

The smell of the big cats struck Jane first. They were penned in an iron cage that had to be far too small for them. Jane had never had a reason to give much thought to the conditions in which wild animals were kept in the shows that toured the country, but she realized Betty was lucky in comparison. A fearsome lion lay with his head on his paws, his eyes following her with little sign of interest. His coat looked dull and, in truth, a little moth-eaten. A lioness was sleeping on her back, one paw delicately touching her chest and twitching occasionally with her dream. Was she dreaming of the wide plains of Africa, Jane wondered, like in the travellers' tales? Of unscaled mountain ranges and thick jungles of knotted vines where there were no paths? Was it better to hope the lion pair had only ever known captivity so did not know what they missed?

"*Capitano*," called Brandon, "I have a visitor for you."

A man popped his head out of another wagon, his face lathered with shaving foam.

"*Un momento!*" he replied.

Before many moments had passed, the lion tamer jumped

down the little stepladder that led from his wagon. He was now dressed in a splendid red jacket of military cut, and his face, cleared of soap, revealed a wonderful pair of winged moustaches, long sideburns, and clean-shaven cheeks. A little curl was shaped on his forehead with the rest swept back. He looked familiar but Jane couldn't place him. She had certainly never to her knowledge met him before.

"*Signorina*, how may I help you?" he asked.

"Sir." Jane dipped a curtsey. "I am seeking to solve a mystery concerning something that went missing at the weekend. My friend here said you remembered an act from the Haymarket that featured a parrot that had been trained to steal shiny items?"

He held up his index finger. "No. Not trained to steal. Trained to fetch."

Jane supposed that was a deliberate distinction because English society tended to look down on theatrical folk and accuse them of all sorts of bad behaviour. "Trained to *fetch*. I was wondering, could you describe the two ladies who ran that show?"

"Please." He swept his hand to a couple of upturned barrels arranged as his makeshift parlour. Jane sat down, hoping she wouldn't be gaining the mark of the rim on the back of her muslin for her politeness. Cassandra would scold her so. "This was a long time ago, in the days of my father, you understand?"

Jane nodded.

"He was the first Capitano Intrepido – the first lion tamer in my family." The man thumped his chest.

He paused, so Jane thought she should add something.

"I see. Then you are also Capitano Intrepido?"

"*Si*, Capitano Intrepido Junior."

He clearly expected something more from her. Light dawning,

Jane got out her notebook and wrote it down. That seemed to satisfy him. "Junior," she repeated solemnly.

Grinning, Brandon also took a seat on a barrel to listen.

"My father," said the lion tamer, "he was a good friend of the Hackitt Sisters. They trained under the same master, the great animal handler, Henri Le Brave."

Jane wrote that down too.

"Miss Hackitt and Miss Rose Hackitt, they specialized in – how you say? – the little creatures, the dogs, the birds, the ponies?"

"The domestic creatures. No cats?" asked Jane.

He looked surprised. "But of course not! Everybody knows you cannot train the little cat; you only tame the big ones and that is very difficult."

"I see." Jane decided she should regard the farmyard cat with more respect in future, as it was one of a species that withstood all human attempts to persuade it to do what they wanted.

"See Abbronzato there?" continued the tamer. "He may look quiet but he would eat you if you went near him."

"I believe you," said Jane.

"Every day I risk my life to prove myself his master. I have my whip and my wits. So far I have won."

The lion yawned, displaying his teeth. Jane got the distinct impression the winning was very much at the lion's pleasure rather than due to anything his trainer did.

"Erm, congratulations." Jane felt they were drifting away from her topic.

"But even worse is his wife! Abbronzato is lazy. La Signora Caterina, she will creep up and leap on you from behind." He clapped his hands. "Thus, you are dead!"

"How splendid," said Jane, noting this down, even though it wasn't the information she was after. Lady Catherine. Sudden leaps. You never knew when it might come in useful.

Capitano Intrepido seemed a little put out that Jane hadn't screamed or fainted like most girls would on hearing of their risk of demise. "You understand? She is deadly? Very, very scary?"

"Yes, I do. I was just thinking that that must make her an excellent hunter, leaping in to defend her family. Capitano Intrepido, I was wondering if you had a description, or any more details about the Hackitt Sisters?"

He pulled a long face. "I am sorry. I saw them once only, when I was very young. Both were very beautiful ladies in their twenties."

"Dark complexion? Light?"

"Hair of the brown, and eyes of the brown too."

Which meant they were like most of women in England. "Any distinguishing characteristics?"

He shrugged. "Not then, but I did hear that the elder, Miss Sarah Hackitt, met with an unfortunate accident." He clutched his heart. "My father, he never forgave himself."

Jane's ears pricked up. "What kind of accident?"

"He had this old lion. He was very bad tempered – the lion, not my father. One night backstage, this lion, he struck out at the lady and caught her here." He tapped his calf.

"A lion bit off Miss Hackitt's leg?" Jane's eyes rounded in amazement.

"Not bit off!" he said indignantly. "The lion, he scratched her, only that, but unfortunately the wound went bad. The blood, it was poisoned, and the poor lady had to have the leg removed to save her life. Ai-eee, so much bad luck from one little cat scratch." He shook his head sadly. Jane herself didn't consider anything coming from a lion's claw as little. "The last my father knew, the Hackitt Sisters had retired from performing and taken up another profession."

Jane thought she knew where. "Do you know what the unfortunate lady is doing now?"

He twirled his moustache pensively. "No, but I would like to know that she is well. The family honour is at stake."

"Oh, I think I can say she is probably doing very well," said Jane, closing her notebook.

Seeing that she was preparing to leave, he stood up. "You know the lady?"

"I might." She thought of the headmistress's miniatures. Had the man in the red coat been the lion tamer's father? Was that from where Jane had recognized him?

He bowed. "Then tell her she will always have free entry to any show that Capitano Intrepido is part of."

"Thank you, Capitano, I will," said Jane, steering a wide path around the sleeping lions, Brandon following on a step behind. Jane knew even if she did find an occasion to pass on the invitation, it seemed unlikely the victim of a lion's scratch would get any enjoyment from attending a show dedicated to the creature that had maimed her.

Back in Sanjay's wagon, Brandon chuckled to himself. "Madame La Tournelle is really Miss Sarah Hackitt! How funny!"

"Yes, it would appear so." Jane underlined the information in her notebook.

"Will you tell her you know her secret?"

Jane tapped the page, pondering. "I'm not sure it is my place to do so. No one believes she is French, so her name is not taken seriously. She is doing no one harm by pretending otherwise."

"But she is using a false name." Brandon ran his hand over his scalp, trying to puzzle his way through the morality of pretending to be someone you were not.

"I imagine she regards it somewhat like a nom de plume or stage name. It is a sad truth that most parents do not think a career as a circus performer fits you for a life as a schoolteacher." Jane could think of no better training than animal tamer for most challenges that happened in a classroom. It was just a shame that Madame had not learned her school lessons better, and what she did know she kept to herself and left the teaching to hirelings. Jane would love to have left school knowing how to train dogs (see her attempts with Grandison) or even birds. Her relationship with the family hens was erratic, to say the least. Every attempt to collect eggs was regarded as a personal assault on their feathered majesties.

Thinking of birds flying the coop…

"Oh Brandon, you probably don't know the news." And she proceeded to tell him about Mr Willoughby's elopement with Lucy Palmer.

Brandon looked shocked. He for one also had not noticed anything going on between the two lovers and said as much. "Mr Willoughby? But why?"

"Lucy wrote that they were heading for Gretna Green – that's a village just over the border with Scotland where you can get married if you are under age without a guardian's permission. Lucy is seventeen, so if she wished to marry in England Mr Warren would have to give his approval."

Brandon shook his head in bewilderment. "But I don't understand: Mr Willoughby had grand plans to settle here and build on his reputation as a dancing master. The old dancing teacher had recently retired so he thought he was on to a good thing."

"My belief is that Lucy persuaded him they could build something better with what she could offer. Did you not notice how she was everywhere at school, listening, watching?"

"I am afraid I barely know the young lady – I did not really notice her."

Jane did not want to examine why she was very pleased he had not paid attention to Lucy. "Exactly! She is very good at what she does. I think she fell for Mr Willoughby – easy enough to do, as he is a handsome man who dances, the two requirements for most girls to fall in love. She also had a special reason why she wanted to leave."

"Which was?" asked Brandon.

"The end of her comfortable berth with the Warrens. Deepti thinks they are in money trouble."

Brandon nodded. "Yes, your friend already told me. Perhaps that is why they are so upset about the loss of the necklace? Could it be all they had left was tied up in Miss Warren's jewels?"

"Maybe. I wonder." Jane had her own theory, but she was keeping that to herself for the moment. "Will you be all right if I leave you here?"

He smiled. "I will do very well with these people. I fit in with them and they have all sworn an oath to protect me. I might even stay with the circus if Mr Willoughby is truly gone. But I would prefer to stay without having to hide from the law."

Jane picked up her shawl. "We'll do our best to clear your name, I promise. I had better get back to Cassandra. My sister is usually very good with younger girls, but I have left her on her own so long that even *her* temper might have cracked."

Jane found Cassandra dragging two girls out of the shallows of the river where they claimed they were collecting interesting weeds. It was clear they were just enjoying paddling. Normally Jane would be on their side, but with eight other girls to keep an eye on, having two in the river was two too many.

The Austen sisters led the slightly damp girls back to school with the promise of buns bought at Deepti and Arjun's bakery.

"Did you find out anything exciting?" asked Cassandra as the girls twittered at the bakery counter, testing Deepti's patience as they struggled to decide between the treats on sale. The look Deepti gave Jane said she was pleased for the custom but really…? So many at once?

Jane shrugged and Deepti laughed.

"Jane? Tell me: did you discover anything of note?" said Cassandra.

Jane smiled mysteriously. "I did."

"And will you tell me?"

"I will."

Cassandra knew she was teasing so didn't rise to the bait as she might otherwise have done. "Good. When?"

Jane picked a coconut pyramid for her own treat and offered the coins to pay for it but Deepti refused.

"Jane!" Cassandra was losing patience.

Jane grinned and relented. "As soon as we've delivered our flock safely back to the pen. But I'll tell you this much now: I know the true identity of Madame La Tournelle and why she only has one leg to stand on."

A Letter in Rhyme

Dear Henry,

In Reading's fair town a lady arrived

And turned herself French with accent contrived.

What strange fate had she we all did wonder,

To have one leg put from her asunder,

And parrot companion with calls bizarre

To raise the curtain and summon the stars?

Was she a pirate who once sailed the seas

In company of buccaneering shes?

Or gone for soldier to follow her man

Right into the guns when the others ran?

But no! A story more odd is at last revealed

A circus life was her beginner's field

Till lion claw rendered leg to lack it

And her true name is unveiled as Sarah Hackitt.

Yours affectionately,

Jane

Chapter 18

Sometime later, while alone in their room, Cassandra showed
Jane the letter from home that had arrived with the afternoon
postbag. It must have crossed with Jane's letter in rhyme that
she had just despatched to Henry – the same postboy carrying
off the letter after delivering this one.

"Mother is asking when we plan to return." Cassandra
tapped her lips with her index finger. "What shall I say? Madame
hasn't asked us to leave, but she has strongly hinted that we
might want to explore educational opportunities somewhere
else now the ball is over."

Jane finished making notes in her book. "She just doesn't
want us sticking our noses into this investigation. She must
also suspect Don Pedro had a hand in the theft and doesn't
want people to start asking where the parrot picked up its
criminal ways."

Tucking the letter in her pocket to be answered later,
Cassandra set out her watercolours to begin colouring the
sketch she had made of Jane earlier that week. "Do you think
it as serious as that?" She dipped the brush into a jar of water.

Jane peered at the sketch from across the worktable. "You've made my bottom too big. You know I'm a beanpole."

Cassandra smirked. "I did not. You are just sitting down with your skirts bunched around you."

Jane tutted. "Not your best likeness. Speaking of which, you know Madame as well as anyone does. Has it not changed your view of her to know her origins?"

"I suppose it does explain the mismatch between her name and her profession. Her manner has always been a trifle odd." Cassandra hummed a little over the paints and then chose blue for Jane's gown.

"Everyone finding out that she is really Sarah Hackitt, circus performer, would put the final nail in the coffin of this school." Jane made a new list of things they had to do in their investigation. "Its fate already hangs by a thread. I'm surprised Mr Warren hasn't taken Elinor and Marianne away already, after the theft. If they go, I imagine many other parents would follow."

Cassandra swirled the brush in the paint to intensify the colours. "Do you think so? From what I've seen, many parents abandon their girls at school and don't pay much more attention to them until the time they are old enough to wed."

Jane looked up in amazement. "A cynical speech from Cassandra – I will make a note in my diary! It must be a blue moon."

"You know I'm only telling the truth."

Jane smiled sadly. "Indeed. I want to ask the parents who do that, why have children if you only think of them as problems to be solved by passing them on to someone else – a school or a husband?"

Cassandra switched to a pale brown for the bonnet in the

sketch – the very one now permanently handed over to Betty. "It would be very sad for the girls I spent time with today if the school were to close. Their friends here are for many of them the only family they know. It's not a comfortable life, but it is what they have grown used to and would miss."

Jane reached out and patted her sister's hand. "Don't worry: we're trying to clear Brandon's name, not close down the school."

Cassandra met her eyes. "What if the two end up being the same thing?"

Wandering around the school after dinner, Jane had to allow that her sister's question was a good one. Jane suspected that the thief she had seen mentioned on the reward posters was none other than Don Pedro. It was summer. People did not think to close windows on upper storeys. What wonderful pickings there must have been for a parrot drawn to shiny items. Had he been ferrying them back to the oak tree, his pirate cave? If so, who had been cleaning out the hollow? The only items left, when the boys from Dr Valpy's climbed up, were a teaspoon and a brass button. Madame seemed an unlikely accomplice, due to her injury that made tree-climbing an impossibility.

There was one possible source of information – the parrot himself.

Jane found him perched on a mirror in the ballroom, bending over from time to time to admire himself. She had come prepared and scattered on the ground in front of her some peanuts borrowed from the jar in Madame's study.

"Don Pedro, curtain up!" she called.

Hearing one of his favourite phrases, the parrot abandoned

his reflection and glided to land at her feet. Now, how to question an avian suspect? Jane had never faced such a challenge before. She supposed it would be somewhat like asking Grandison questions – a lot of interpretation on her part and some goodwill necessary on his.

She tried out some words. "Haymarket? Peanuts. Beginners please."

"Curtain up!" said Don Pedro in an interested tone, his head to one side.

"Sarah Hackitt?"

"Sarah, who's a lovely boy, Sarah," the parrot chattered.

It was some proof that he knew the name Sarah already. She tried again.

"Sarah Hackitt?"

"Sarah, Sarah, Sarah and Rosie."

Rosie? Was that the sister? The lion tamer had said that was her name, hadn't he?

"Where's Rosie?" she tried.

But the parrot was only trained to repeat sounds; he didn't understand them. He cocked his head the other way. "Beginners, please."

She shelled him another nut and offered it to him. With a rare display of politeness, he took it in his beak and flew back to the mirror. The next step would be to find Rosie – and Jane suspected she needed to go no further than to the kitchen for that.

There was little to be gained by marching straight in and asking her questions. Besides, the women inside were busy and would be very unlikely to talk in front of her. Lurking in the corridor with the brushes and mops, peeking around the door, Jane found Matron Brown, the cook, and the scullery maid all sharing the washing-up duty. There was a lot of it for a school of girls and no sign of other staff. The three women made an interesting contrast: Matron tiny and delicate, Cook stout like a washerwoman, and the maid willow-wand tall, though her shoulders stooped.

"I don't know how much more of this I can take," said Matron Brown in her soft voice. She sounded close to tears as she ferried the dirty dishes to the basin. "I did not agree to become a kitchen skivvy when I took on this post."

The kitchen maid slammed a pot on the drainer. "I am the skivvy, but I didn't think I'd have to do all the work meself. What's happened to Ben and Martin? Why don't we have help anymore?"

The cook heaved up the washed pot and set it on the warm oven. "Shut your complaining, you two. You know how things stand. Madame did you both a favour taking you in when no one else would offer you a position."

The maid huffed, slopping water over the floor. "I wouldn't mind if I got paid regular."

Cook flicked a drying cloth at her. "You will be, Ruth. Just be patient. Temporary difficulties. You know how it is?"

"It seems to have been like that for years," said Matron gloomily. "Why don't we train us up a new bird or two, and dogs? I used to love Auntie's dogs." Having ferried the dirty crockery to the sink, she started putting the clean away. "They were so clever, dancing to music and climbing on boxes."

"It ain't that easy, Jenny," said Cook. "An act like what we used to have takes years to create. And you don't have the stage presence to front an act. You should've seen your aunt in her heyday!" Cook's eyes went misty with the memory before she shook herself. "Besides, we've only got Don Pedro left and he's more of a liability than a circus act these days."

Jane crammed herself back in a corner as Matron passed close to her on her way to the kitchen dresser. "Do you think he did it? Stole the necklace?" asked Matron.

The cook shushed her. "Keep your voice down! We mustn't speak of that!"

"But that poor boy is being blamed. It isn't right!"

"Who is to say he didn't train the bird to bring the necklace to him?" The cook didn't sound too convinced by her own explanation. "With a few peanuts as bribes, Don Pedro can usually be persuaded to do what you want."

"But when would the boy have had the chance to bribe the bird?" countered Matron. "He was only here once or twice for the ball rehearsals."

Jane agreed with Matron – that had never made any sense.

"Then maybe that Willoughby did it?" said Cook, a snarl in her voice. "He was always in and out giving his lessons, smiling, bending and bowing, thinking he was the cat's whiskers. Never liked him – a tricky customer, that one." The cook folded her arms under her ample bust, rosy cheeks flushed. "I used to meet lots of men like that at the Haymarket when I was a girl. They looked pretty enough but were rotten at the core. No moral fibre."

Excited to have her answer, Jane retreated. But she had forgotten exactly where she was and bumped against the mop and pail. She watched in horror as the handle arced to the floor and landed with a clatter.

The conversation in the kitchen ceased immediately.

"Who's out there?" The cook took a step toward the door.

Just then, Don Pedro, who must have followed Jane, swooped in, squawking: "Peanuts. Peanuts. Beginners please."

"It's just that dratted bird," said Cook. "Don Pedro, you'll end up as parrot stew one day if you keep on scaring me like that." She flapped her apron at him.

Jane breathed a sigh of relief – quietly – and crept away.

With no more clues to follow up for the present, Jane kept watch on the comings and goings at the school. The Bow Street Runner appeared mid-morning and marched straight in to Madame La Tournelle's study. He stayed for only fifteen minutes before he strode out again, this time carrying Don Pedro in his cage. *What is he going to do with the bird?* Jane wondered. He could hardly arrest it.

Next to leave was Madame herself. There was something about the furtive way she looked back at the school that alerted Jane to her shady intentions.

Jane glanced at Cassandra, who was deep in a novel she had borrowed from Marianne.

"I'm going to follow Madame; do you want to come?"

"Hmm," said Cassandra. She wasn't really listening.

"I'm going to fly to the moon."

"All right. See you later."

There was nothing quite like an Austen with a new novel. You could let off a cannon beside them and they would not flinch.

Throwing a shawl around her shoulders and cramming her hair under an old bonnet of her sister's, Jane hurried out. Grandison tried to accompany her, but she shut the door on him with a whispered apology. The dog, for one, would be pleased when they got home; he was being shut out of adventures far too often. She passed Marianne in the ballroom teaching the younger girls to bat. That did not look promising for the windows. Elinor was walking dreamily in the garden, hand brushing the tops of the roses. She lifted a handkerchief to dab away a tear. Was she crying over her diamonds, her father's predicament, or the absent Willoughby? Perhaps all three?

Hurrying, Jane slipped out of the gate and caught up with Madame La Tournelle as she turned into the High Street. She didn't stop at any of the shops in the marketplace but carried on until she came to a dingy alleyway. Pausing, the headmistress took a careful look around. Jane dived behind the town pump. Madame La Tournelle then proceeded down the alley. When Jane reached the entrance, she saw her turn into a shop with the distinctive three balls sign, marking it out as a pawnbroker.

Had it been Madame all along? Was she retrieving the necklace she had already pawned for money, or even pledging it now? No, surely not! It would be too recognizable. There were posters about it on every street corner with reward notices. Jane crept nearer and crouched by the door. It had not closed fully behind the headmistress, so fragments of the conversation reached Jane.

"Sarah, I cannot keep taking these things from you," said the pawnbroker in a husky voice. "Someone is going to recognize their things."

"I've explained. These are chance found goods. They don't belong to anyone." Madame La Tournelle's accent was her London one, suggesting the pawnbroker was well aware of her origins. "I didn't steal them. Do you arrest a magpie for its fondness for shiny objects?"

Jane thought that the defence of "the parrot did it" was not going to wash in court. The pawnbroker appeared to share her opinion.

"It's too risky," he said. "I just can't."

"Not if you send it to Jarvis in Covent Garden again. No one will trace it back to here. He can be trusted."

There was a sigh. "You're sailing close to the wind, Sarah."

"Like old times, isn't it?" Madame sounded almost amused. There was the soul of a pirate in her even if she'd never sailed the Seven Seas, thought Jane. "When have I ever set a different course? It's got me this far and I'm not giving up now."

There was a rattle as the cash box was pulled out. "Three guineas. That's my final offer and the last time, agreed?"

"Thank you, Joe. I knew I could rely on you. You're a good man." Jane risked a peek around the door. Madame was patting him on the cheek and then pocketing the coins in the purse on her girdle. "Now I can pay the butcher."

The pawnbroker was a big man with the weathered complexion of one who had spent many years outside, perhaps as a shepherd, sailor, or soldier. Now he was shaking his head at himself. "Humph! Last time, remember? The good old times only go so far."

"I remember." But there was something in her tone that suggested she wouldn't pay any attention.

As Madame La Tournelle turned to leave, Jane crammed herself back into a doorway further along the alleyway. The headmistress exited the shop. Once she'd hopped her way out of sight, Jane went back to the pawnbroker's and looked through the dusty window. She wasn't expecting to see a diamond necklace put out in plain sight, but she wanted to gauge what manner of goods he handled. A metal grille protected the glass. On the counter lay a strange collection of items pledged by their desperate owners. If you were short of ready money you could leave your valuables with the broker in exchange for cash. He gave you time to return for them once you had the coin plus some interest to pay for the lending service. If you didn't go back, he was free to sell your pledged item. The things on sale were those that people had not returned for: brooches, rings, a snuff box, a trumpet. That last was sad. What if it belonged to a desperate musician who could now no longer earn their living?

Don't be so gloomy, Jane scolded herself. Perhaps the player had lacked all talent and this was a blessed relief for friends and family? She then remembered Brandon had had to flee without his flute. Perhaps she should see what had become of it?

The door opened and the pawnbroker came out.

"Can I help you, Miss?" His tone was only just respectful as he tried to gauge if she were customer or nuisance. His upright bearing and scar down the left cheek made Jane suspect he was a former soldier.

"I was just curious," said Jane.

"Then I suggest you take your curiosity somewhere else. Be off with you!" He made a shooing gesture.

"And good day to you too, sir," said Jane in a tone that would've earned a scolding from her mother. But Mama wasn't here and this man dealt in stolen goods. He did not deserve better from her.

Walking away, Jane further considered the conversation she had overheard. Three guineas were nowhere near the value of a diamond earring, let alone a necklace. That suggested Madame's transactions were much more in the way of the smaller thefts made by the burglar parrot. Jane could imagine Joe and this Jarvis in London had a tidy arrangement where stolen items from both towns were swapped between them and then put up for sale far from where they had gone missing. It was a good plan – not good in the moral sense but as a way of hiding your activities. Jane also admired their cunning, until she thought of the victims. Don Pedro was no Robin Hood. He took indiscriminately, and, though Madame selling the items meant a school of girls got fed, perhaps some other family was going hungry?

Chapter 19

When Jane neared the school, she considered her next steps. In her opinion, it was fairly firmly established that the parrot had taken the necklace and that the theft had not been a planned event but someone taking advantage of the fact that Don Pedro had made the necklace into – what had Madame said? – a "chance found thing". The most obvious contender for the person to exploit the situation was the headmistress, as she already had a system in place to shift stolen goods. However, it was unlikely that Madame had had a moment to go wandering around the Forbury in hopes of discovering where the thieving parrot had stowed it, not when she had a whole school in uproar at her summer ball, with numerous guests and a great number of crises to handle. It made more sense to suggest that someone else knew about the parrot and slipped away as soon as they heard what had been taken. Logically, that was most likely to be someone who spent the majority of her time in the school, aware of all the comings and goings, including the habits of the resident parrot. Jane had sniffed out Madame's past after only a few days. As Cassandra had annoyingly pointed out, Lucy Palmer was somewhat like Jane in her curiosity and she had had a head start. When everyone else had been distracted by Elinor's bombshell of news about the theft, had Lucy immediately understood what had happened and been first in the field? Or, in this case, up a tree?

This thought made Jane feel slightly more at ease with making an accusation. Lucy was family. The Warrens would keep any punishment a private affair. No judge, jury, and executioner would be called in, not like if poor Brandon had been put on trial.

As Jane approached the gatehouse, Cassandra hurried out to meet her, ribbons on her cap fluttering.

"Jane, you'll never guess what has happened!"

"Lucy Palmer has returned unwed and without Mr Willoughby?" suggested Jane.

Cassandra's jaw dropped. "What! How did you know?"

"I didn't know, I only guessed. Am I right?"

"Yes! Lucy turned up at the school not half an hour ago. Madame was out, which was fortunate I suppose for her, but the cook took over and marched Lucy home to the Warrens' house to face her uncle."

Jane didn't envy Lucy that encounter. It was hard for any girl to regain her reputation once it was known she had run away with a man. To return married sometimes helped mend the damage – flaunt a wedding ring and many people pretended to forget how you came by it. But to return still unwed was a disaster. Lucy would probably get sent off to some tough old aunt in the countryside and never be allowed out in society again.

"You seem not to be surprised. What do you think happened after they left?" asked Cassandra.

Jane thought her way through the steps. "I'll wager that Lucy and Mr Willoughby stopped off at the first big town after Reading to pawn the necklace. They might even have gone to London to do so, and not Gretna Green. Lucy's note was probably just to send any pursuers on a wild goose chase."

"Indeed. How mortifying it will be to discover no pursuit was mounted. Our father and brothers would all be on horseback with no delay if either of us took it into our heads to elope."

Jane squeezed her sister's hand. "I know. That's because we have a loving family behind us. I do feel sorry for Lucy for not having that."

"Then what do you think happened in London?"

"I think they were told that their marvellous stolen ticket to future prosperity was in fact paste jewels and only worth a modest sum for their decorative value. You have to admit that they were very good fakes, after all. What the necklace would have fetched might've been enough to pay for the coach trip to Scotland, but not for the start in life Lucy had promised her beau. Once Mr Willoughby learned this, he realized the full idiocy of his actions. He'd made a good start in Reading and thrown it all up for the dream of something better. My guess is he left her, is probably on the first ship to France or America, and regrets the day he ever fell for a tolerably pretty girl with her cunning plan."

Cassandra shook her head in amazement at her sister's farsightedness. "How do you know they were paste?"

Jane was delighted to impress her sister. "It is logical. Think about it. Did it not worry you that a lowly girls' school should host such valuables? Why leave them here in advance of the ball at all, placed only in a trunk that spent some time unattended in the hallway, not to mention sitting for hours in a bedroom with only a lock on the door? That suggested they weren't truly concerned for them but wanted them here in advance to advertise Elinor's vast wealth. If they were worth a fortune, Mr Warren could have sent the diamonds that very evening and had a stout footman on hand to check his daughters were not accosted when decked out in such finery."

"That is true," said Cassandra with the pensive expression Jane loved so much. It wrinkled her forehead in a very solemn manner.

"And didn't you think it odd that Elinor wanted to wear them in the first place? She was clearly overdressed for the company, which is not very good manners if you think about it."

"It's not?" asked Cassandra.

"When we visit the farmers' wives, we don't wear our best clothes but our most practical so as not to make them feel awkward in our presence. Elinor dressed as if she were going to a ball at Windsor with the king."

"Then why dress like that?"

Jane smiled at her sister. "Because it was the one event in the year when she could impress notions of her wealth on all the young men of her class – perhaps not the boys from Dr Valpy's themselves, but their brothers and uncles who would hear rumours of the Indian heiress and her dowry of maharajah's jewels. It sounds like a fairy tale but I think Elinor is very practical underneath it all. She is trying to help her family by marrying well and, like a peacock, she is using a flamboyant display to catch her mate. The reason the Warrens were so devastated to lose the jewels was that their true financial straits would be revealed. They couldn't have been more worried if the diamonds were real – oh!"

This last exclamation was on finding Marianne in their

bedchamber, waiting for them with her arms around Grandison. She would've overheard that last remark.

"Mine are real," said Marianne despondently. "It is Elinor's set we had to sell."

"Marianne, I'm sorry. It must be very distressing for you," said Cassandra, embracing the younger girl.

Marianne's voice was muffled in the hug. "It is. Instead of launching ourselves successfully in Reading, we have ended up disgraced. And we'll have to leave, and I'll never get to play cricket again or live near Edward."

That was an odd line up of priorities, but Jane could allow her some confusion in her distress. "Why do you have to leave?" asked Jane. "No one blames you for Lucy's choices."

Moving back from Cassandra, Marianne waved that away. "This isn't about our cousin but our money – or lack of it."

Jane sat down on the bed beside her. "Who has to know?"

"What?" Marianne looked up.

"There are whispers, that is true, but most people are gossiping about the dangerously handsome dancing master and Lucy's scandalous attempt to run away. No one else knows the reason for her return. She could just say she had second thoughts before it went too far and ran back home to beg forgiveness."

"That is her best choice," agreed Cassandra on Marianne's other side.

"And if she agrees to keep quiet about the fake diamonds, perhaps your father could find somewhere for her that would not be so dire a future as seclusion in the countryside with whatever aunt he is lining up right now?" suggested Jane.

"Great-Aunt Norris. She's a dragon," said Marianne.

"You must have some money, enough to establish her

somewhere far away from this scandal?" asked Jane.

"It is the duty of a Christian to give people a second chance if they ask forgiveness," said Cassandra softly.

"I'm not sure she is repentant, more that she is furious she took a gamble and lost," said Marianne, wisely guessing her cousin's state of mind.

"I merely think it is too melodramatic for everyone to throw their hands up in the air and announce you are all doomed when a quiet settlement could spare everyone any blushes," said Jane.

Marianne bit her lip, ruminating on what had been said. "You know, I think you are right. I should go home and talk to Papa. I don't think he'll listen to me though."

"Then take Elinor. She seems very astute and you said he listens to her."

Marianne smiled sadly. "Ah, you realize that about her now, do you? She is more like me than we both pretend. I mean that in sisters you rarely find one has all the sense and the other all the sensibility. Both of us can be very practically minded when we try."

Jane got up and held out a hand. "Do you want us to come with you?"

"Would you? I think we could do with the moral support."

"Of course – and I haven't even taken my bonnet off so I'm ready to go. Only Miss Impulsive here who ran outside as soon as she saw me needs to get properly dressed." Jane shooed Cassandra to the hatstand.

They fetched Elinor from her room, and the four girls made their way through Reading to Edward's house. This was a smart town residence on the main road out to London. He rented a set of rooms at the top, but the rest of the house had been taken for his father while he was in England. A carriage was waiting outside, already summoned to dispatch the disgraced girl to the dragon aunt. The coachman and footmen looked like gaolers, thought Jane, iron-faced and muscled like boxers. Lucy wouldn't be slipping away from these men.

The girls didn't wait to be announced by the butler but went straight into the room Mr Warren had commandeered as his study. Already present were Edward, Mr Warren, Mr Jennings, and Lucy. She was standing in front of the fireplace, wringing her hands, her head held up in defiance. Pink-cheeked and dressed in white, she did a very good impression of a fragile female defending her honour against wild accusations. However, in this case, the accusations happened to be true.

"I don't believe you!" Mr Warren shouted. "Of all the preposterous defences: a parrot took it!"

The Bow Street Runner took out his notebook. "I do believe the young woman might be telling the truth, sir. The school owns a larcenous parrot by the name of Don Pedro. I confiscated him yesterday to test his skills, and he has already stolen six brass buttons and a silver fork from the lodging house where I am staying."

Mr Warren flushed an alarming purple with anger. "All right. I'll grant this ridiculous story, but that doesn't change what you chose to do next, Lucy! You must have known that was Elinor's necklace, and yet you pocketed it, pretended to be concerned for your cousin, allowed another person to be accused, all the while plotting to run off with that foolish dancing master!" Mr Warren looked up and saw the four girls had entered. "See, they all know! This is a disaster for you, young miss, but also for my daughters. Did you think of them at all when you ran away?"

Lucy folded her arms, a hint of temper sparking. She

appeared to have decided to go down with guns blazing, which made Jane like her better for it. "Think of them? Of course I thought of them. I thought how they had everything, and I have nothing. I thought how we were all set to stay in this backwater of a town without even a decent ballroom or assembly rooms, when we could make so many more impressive connections, like in London or Bath. When I joined your household, that was the future I imagined. Then I heard that your own fortunes were on the edge of a knife, likely as not to fall, and I thought I had to seize my one chance to establish myself happily with the man I loved."

"And how worthy of your love was this man?" sneered Mr Warren.

"Not at all," said Lucy, brushing a tear away with her wrist. "I'm glad I didn't marry him."

Silence fell. It was the Bow Street Runner who broke it.

"Do you want me to arrest the young woman on the charge of receiving stolen goods?"

Mr Warren broke out of his deep thoughts. "What? No! She's a Warren, even if she doesn't bear our surname. That is one small mercy in this debacle. We'll deal with this as a family matter." He then realized they had a stranger in their midst who might well carry tales back to London. He dug in his pocket and handed over a bag of coins to the Runner. "Here is your fee, Jennings. You may go now."

The man scowled. "But a crime was committed."

"By a parrot," said Jane, inserting herself between the Bow Street man and the master of the house. "I doubt any magistrate would like to rule on this."

Mr Jennings looked thoughtful. He hadn't seen the implications of turning up in court with a suspect with a beak and feathers. He would become a laughing stock.

Jane seized her moment: he just needed a nudge out of the door, a new scent to follow. "However, I did come across some evidence that there is a connection between a pawnbroker's just off the market square and a Mr Jarvis in London: that might be a case worthy of your time?" Jane suggested.

Everyone looked at her in surprise. True, a girl in a grubby-hemmed muslin dress didn't seem a likely person to have unearthed such a plot, but then it was often the ones sitting in the corner overlooked who saw the most.

"Jarvis, you say? I know him. He works on my patch in Covent Garden." Mr Jennings's eyes brightened. "So this is where he's been sending his ill-gotten goods, is it?" He rubbed his hands together. "Well, well, well. Thank you, young miss, I'll look into that before I head back to town." Patting his pocket to ensure that his fee was safely stowed, Mr Jennings bowed to the company and departed for the market square.

Cassandra waggled her brows at Jane, who mouthed that she would tell her later how she had come by such unexpected intelligence.

"Will you reveal what passed here?" Mr Warren asked the Austen sisters uneasily.

"Us?" Jane touched her breast. "No! And besides, we know no one in society but live quietly in a village in Hampshire. We are, and will remain, quite obscure, nobody knowing our name. We are not a threat to you."

"Then I will send Lucy away to my Aunt Norris and draw a veil over the whole sorry affair," he said with an air of finality.

But Lucy was not going to allow that to be her fate, and she fought back the best way she could. "If you do that, I'll write to the newspapers – tell them how you lost half the army payroll on a bad bet and had to use your own family money to make up the shortfall." Lucy's tone was acid.

So that was what had happened, thought Jane, the last puzzle piece of the mystery revealed. He had gambled money that wasn't his to risk. That was stealing of a kind, Jane thought, aware of the irony even if no one else in the room dared point it out. Mr Warren would be dismissed from his role as Collector if it came out he wasn't very good at keeping that which he had collected.

"Ungrateful girl!" he fumed.

"Might I suggest, Father, that you send Lucy to school in Dublin instead? You have cousins there with a large family of girls. She would enjoy the companionship and her misstep wouldn't follow her so far as to Ireland," Elinor said quietly, laying a hand on his arm. How had Jane missed how very managing Elinor was in her own way? No wonder father and daughter were so close: they were conspirators in this scheme to keep the Warren name out of the scandal sheets.

"Why should I do that?" he growled.

"Because she would have something to lose. Send her to Aunt Norris and she would do anything desperate to escape."

Jane nodded in fervent agreement. *Just so!*

He frowned and played with his watch chain for a moment, studying the problem from the angle Elinor suggested.

"Very well. Lucy shall go to Dublin and stay with the Kennedys. If she lets one hint of this slip, she will find herself with Aunt Norris before she knows what has hit her."

"I think that a good plan, Father," said Edward, speaking up for the first time. "I'll take a few days' leave of absence and take her there myself. That way we can ensure there are no more mistakes."

"Lucy, do you like this plan?" asked Elinor, stepping up again as the family arbitrator.

Lucy threw up her hands. "Of course I like it. Anything is better than Aunt Norris." She wasn't showing much gratitude, but then the Lucy Palmers of this world were not naturally grateful creatures, thought Jane. They were ambitious ones, and setbacks such as this would soon be overcome or used as stepping stones to something better. Jane suspected that the dancing masters of Dublin had better be on their guard.

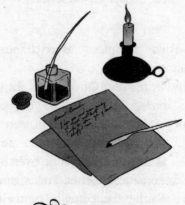

Chapter 20

The game stopped by parrot had resumed on the next fine day. Cassandra was bowling. She had mastered the art of a nasty little spin bowl that often caught out their brothers at home, and now one of Dr Valpy's boys was about to face it. He swung at a ball that had curved under his bat and his bails went flying. The small crowd that had gathered to watch the conclusion of the long-delayed cricket match applauded. Jane, standing in the outfield, jumped up and down with excitement. It was going to be a close match. Thanks to a first wicket stand by Marianne and Edward, Madame La Tournelle's team were ahead by fifty runs, but the boys were fast catching up. The disgraced Mr Willoughby had been replaced by Mr Warren, who had proved to be a much better sport than Jane anticipated. He had even muttered an apology to Brandon, blushing furiously as he did so as it did not come naturally to him to admit he had been wrong. Arjun and Deepti had both made athletic catches, and Jane herself had helped run someone out – unfortunately, it had been a teammate so she hadn't covered the Austen name in glory.

To be honest, not all attention was on the match. Brandon had brought his circus friends to spectate, including Betty the elephant, who was tethered in the shade of the infamous oak tree. She was responsible for drawing the crowd. Don Pedro, released from his cage and warned never to steal again, was perched on her forehead as if this was quite the most natural thing in the world. It now seemed that the parrot would leave with Brandon and the circus, as it had been generally agreed, even by Madame, that he needed an audience for his talent, rather than a town to burglarize.

Michael Redfern and Tom Thatcher were the last pair in to bat. It was all coming down to the final over. If they scored six or more, they would claim victory. Jane did not envy her sister the pressure. Cassandra rubbed the ball on the most practical of her gowns and studied the stout form of Thatcher, defending his wicket. She ran up, and bowled, but Jane could see it was a little short. Thatcher's bat connected and he skied it. If it went over the boundary, the boys would win and Cassandra in particular would feel she were to blame for the defeat. Jane's heart missed a beat.

But help was at hand. Grandison raced after the ball, leaped in the air, and snatched it with his teeth. He then ran hysterically to Jane and spun in a circle, ball still clenched in his jaws.

"Oh, clever dog!" Jane cried.

"Out!" The other girls screamed.

Thatcher said something that sounded very much like "infernal dog" and kicked the bails over, but Jane forgave him the insult as it was the second time Grandison had caused him to be dismissed.

The boys cheered up considerably when they saw the cricket tea had been supplied by Deepti and Arjun. Mr Warren had footed the bill in thanks for the assistance with the diamond burglary. He might have lost a lot of money, but he was still many times richer than Jane's father would ever be in his lifetime. Elinor was right in concluding their remaining wealth would still buy them respect in a place the size of Reading.

Guest of honour at the tea was Betty, who probably had never been fed so many buns in her life. She looked to be thoroughly enjoying the attention and patiently put up with Don Pedro screeching "Beginners please!" from the crown of her head.

There was still one thing Jane felt she should do. Catching the headmistress alone for a moment, Jane had a quiet word with Madame La Tournelle about lost items, a certain pawnbroker, and interest from the Bow Street Runner. Madame paled and quickly changed the subject, declaring Jane quite the cleverest girl who had ever come to her school and a very dear child. Thanks to Mr Warren deciding to keep his daughters in a place where they were so happy, some of Madame's money troubles were over, so she was keen to put the last few rocky months behind her. Jane had even noticed the return of a few more servants to share the load.

"You'll be going home soon, I trust?" Madame said, giving her a nod as if to usher her back to Steventon right away. "Back to your little rectory?"

Jane understood she was really asking how long she would have to put up with Jane's eyes on her back. It was unpleasant to be aware that your shameful secrets were known to someone else.

"We will be gone very soon," said Jane. "But Marianne and Elinor will be writing to us, so they will tell us all your news." Jane hoped that was enough for the headmistress to resist any more "chance found" things. The butcher would have in future to be paid from fees.

As the headmistress walked swiftly away with her uneven gait, Brandon came up to Jane, his flute case in hand. He was heading off with the circus that very day as they continued on their tour of the country. He bowed.

"Thank you, Miss Jane, for clearing my name."

She curtseyed. "Thank you, Mr Brandon, for discovering about the parrot. The investigation would never have uncovered the truth without your enquiries about the famous Hackitt Sisters."

"My pleasure." He gave her a sunny smile, so much happier than when she first met him. He really had found himself a new family, it would appear.

"I also wanted to thank you for helping me when I was having trouble with my dancing," said Jane. "I knew such a kind person could not be guilty of the crimes they alleged."

He shook his head. "That was nothing."

"No, not nothing. You have given me back my love of dancing and that is no small debt I owe you. I will try to thank you one day if I can."

He chuckled. "All right then. I will look out for that thank you."

And Jane vowed, even if their paths did not cross again, she would make sure to send him a message in whatever way she could that he had been a hero to her when she was feeling low.

Cassandra joined them with a plate of cakes and Grandison trotting at her side with hopeful eyes on any crumbs that she might drop.

"Mama has finally sent word, Jane. Henry will fetch us tomorrow."

Jane clapped her hands. "At last."

"I remember having to drag you here. Are you still looking forward to going home, back to books, chores, and stolen plums?" asked Cassandra.

Jane looked around the cricket field with the elephant, parrot, assorted new friends, some vanquished enemies, and the excitement of a place with such a variety of society. Deepti and Marianne were playing catch with a cricket ball; Edward Warren was strolling arm in arm with Elinor. Mr Warren was sitting with Dr Valpy, discussing the news of the day. "Actually, I wouldn't mind staying a bit longer if Mama could spare us. I've not really had time to catch up with Deepti. Shall we send word we are staying to become pastry cooks and delay Henry's arrival?"

Brandon took a bite of a ginger cake. "Definitely stay if it means learning to cook like this."

"Mama would have palpitations if you suggested such a thing." Cassandra looped her arms through Jane's and gave her a friendly jostle.

"Ah well. I suppose there are plenty of things to entertain us both in the countryside – and a lot more time for writing." Jane brightened. This stay had given her so many ideas for stories to entertain her family. She might struggle to include an elephant and a burglar parrot, but there were human characters to imagine in another story – a tale of sisters, duplicitous lovers, and missing money. "Yes, Cassandra, I think I am ready to go home."

Words of the mirror-writing letter from p. 109:

A Reflection on Our Situation

My dear Henry,

Just a quick note dashed off when I heard a messenger was heading your way. Having settled on a chief suspect – Madame's thieving parrot – we hunted high and low. Our search within the Abbey proved fruitless, so we recruited two boys from the neighbouring school to climb Don Pedro's favourite tree. Our hopes were raised when they returned with several teaspoons and an old bangle. Delving deeper, though, the necklace was nowhere to be found.

Were we right to suspect the parrot? It certainly explains the mysterious ability of the thief to pass unseen. Or were we accusing an innocent bird?

None of this matters, as we cannot prove the theory either way. I am quite despondent that we will not be able to help our friend. Perhaps we should think of a way of getting him out of Reading and away to safety?

Your affectionately,

Jane

BOOK ONE OUT NOW!

A young Jane Austen uncovers the mysterious
happenings at Southmoor Abbey.

'A Little Princess - with tigers!'
Ally Sherrick, award-winning author of Black Powder